Francis M. Crawford

Adam Johnstone's Son

Francis M. Crawford

Adam Johnstone's Son

ISBN/EAN: 9783337398576

Printed in Europe, USA, Canada, Australia, Japan

Cover: Foto ©Andreas Hilbeck / pixelio.de

More available books at **www.hansebooks.com**

ADAM JOHNSTONE'S SON

BY

F. MARION CRAWFORD

AUTHOR OF "SARACINESCA," "PIETRO GHISLERI," "KATHARINE
LAUDERDALE," "THE RALSTONS," ETC.

WITH NUMEROUS ILLUSTRATIONS

New York
MACMILLAN AND CO.
LONDON: MACMILLAN & CO., LTD.
1896

CONTENTS

v

LIST OF ILLUSTRATIONS

vii

ADAM JOHNSTONE'S SON

CHAPTER I

"I SOMETIMES think that one's past life is written in a foreign language," said Mrs. Bowring, shutting the book she held, but keeping the place with one smooth, thin forefinger, while her still, blue eyes turned from her daughter's face towards the hazy hills that hemmed the sea thirty miles to the southward. "When one wants to read it, one finds ever so many words which one cannot understand, and one has to look them out in a sort of unfamiliar dictionary, and try to make sense of the sentences as best one can. Only the big things are clear."

Clare glanced at her mother, smiling innocently and half mechanically, without much definite expression, and quite without curiosity. Youth can be in sympathy with age, while not understanding it, while not suspecting, perhaps, that there is anything to understand beyond the streaked hair and the pale glance and the little torture-lines which paint the portrait of fifty years for the eyes of twenty.

B   1

Every woman knows the calendar of her own face. The lines are years, one for such and such a year, one for such and such another; the streaks are months, perhaps, or weeks, or sometimes hours, where the tear-storms have bleached the brown, the black, or the gold. "This little wrinkle — it was so very little then!" she says. "It came when I doubted for a day. There is a shadow there, just at each temple, where the cloud passed, when my sun went out. The bright hair grew lower on my forehead. It is worn away, as though by a crown, that was not of gold. There are hollows there, near the ears, on each side, since that week when love was done to death before my eyes and died — intestate — leaving his substance to be divided amongst indifferent heirs. They wrangle for what he has left, but he himself is gone, beyond hearing or caring, and, thank God, beyond suffering. But the marks are left."

Youth looks on and sees alike the ill-healed wounds of the martyrdom and the rough scars of sin's scourges, and does not understand. Clare Bowring smiled, without definite expression, just because her mother had spoken and seemed to ask for sympathy; and then she looked away for a few moments. She had a bit of work in her hands, a little bag which she was making out of a piece of old Italian damask, to hold a needle-case and thread and scissors. She had stopped sewing, and instinctively waited before beginning again, as though to acknowledge by a little affectionate deference that her mother had said something serious and had a right to expect attention. But she did not answer, for she could not understand.

Her own young life was vividly clear to her; so very vividly clear, that it sometimes made her think of a tiresome chromolithograph. All the facts and thoughts of it were so near that she knew them by heart, as people come to know the patterns of the wall-paper in the room they inhabit. She had nothing to hide, nothing to regret, nothing which she thought she should care very much to recall, though she remembered everything. A girl is very young when she can recollect distinctly every frock she has had, the first long one, and the second, and the third; and the first ball gown, and the second, and no third, because that is still in the future, and a particular pair of gloves which did not fit, and a certain pair of shoes she wore so long because they were so comfortable, and the precise origin of every one of the few trinkets and bits of jewellery she possesses. That was Clare Bowring's case. She could remember everything and everybody in her life. But her father was not in her memories, and there was a little motionless

grey cloud in the place where he should have
been. He had been a soldier, and had been killed
in an obscure skirmish with black men, in one
of England's obscure but expensive little wars.
Death is always very much the same thing, and
it seems unfair that the guns of Balaclava should
still roar "glory" while the black man's quick
spear-thrust only spells "dead," without comment.
But glory in death is even more a matter of luck
than fame in life. At all events, Captain Bowring, as brave a gentleman as ever faced fire,
had perished like so many other brave gentlemen
of his kind, in a quiet way, without any fuss,
beyond killing half a dozen or so of his assail-
ants, and had left his widow the glory of receiv-
ing a small pension in return for his blood, and
that was all. Some day, when the dead are
reckoned, and the manner of their death noted,
poor Bowring may count for more than some of
his friends who died at home from a constitu-
tional inability to enjoy all the good things
fortune set before them, complicated by a disposition incapable of being satisfied with only a
part of the feast. But at the time of this tale
they counted for more than he; for they had
been constrained to leave behind them what
they could not consume, while he, poor man,
had left very little besides the aforesaid interest
in the investment of his blood, in the form of a

pension to his widow, and the small grey cloud in the memory of his girl-child, in the place where he should have been. For he had been killed when she had been a baby.

The mother and daughter were lonely, if not alone in the world; for when one has no money to speak of, and no relations at all, the world is a lonely place, regarded from the ordinary point of view — which is, of course, the true one. They had no home in England, and they generally lived abroad, more or less, in one or another of the places of society's departed spirits, such as Florence. They had not, however, entered into Limbo without hope, since they were able to return to the social earth when they pleased, and to be alive again, and the people they met abroad sometimes asked them to stop with them at home, recognising the fact that they were still socially living and casting shadows. They were sure of half a hundred friendly faces in London and of half a dozen hospitable houses in the country; and that is not little for people who have nothing wherewith to buy smiles and pay for invitations. Clare had more than once met women of her mother's age and older, who had looked at her rather thoughtfully and longer than had seemed quite natural, saying very quietly that her father had been " a great friend of theirs." But those were not the women

whom her mother liked best, and Clare sometimes wondered whether the little grey cloud
in her memory, which represented her father,
might not be there to hide away something
more human than an ideal. Her mother spoke
of him, sometimes gravely, sometimes with a
far-away smile, but never tenderly. The smile
did not mean much, Clare thought. People
often spoke of dead people with a sort of faint
look of uncertain beatitude — the same which
many think appropriate to the singing of hymns.
The absence of anything like tenderness meant
more. The gravity was only natural and decent.

" Your father was a brave man," Mrs. Bowring sometimes said. " Your father was very
handsome," she would say. " He was very
quick-tempered," she perhaps added.

But that was all. Clare had a friend whose
husband had died young and suddenly, and her
friend's heart was broken. She did not speak
as Mrs. Bowring did. When the latter said that
her past life seemed to be written in a foreign
language, Clare did not understand, but she
knew that the something of which the transla-
tion was lost, as it were, belonged to her father.
She always felt an instinctive desire to defend
him, and to make her mother feel more sympathy for his memory. Yet, at the same time,
she loved her mother in such a way as made her

feel that if there had been any trouble, her father must have been in the wrong. Then she was quite sure that she did not understand, and she held her tongue, and smiled vaguely, and waited a moment before she went on with her work.

Besides, she was not at all inclined to argue anything at present. She had been ill, and her mother was worn out with taking care of her, and they had come to Amalfi to get quite well and strong again in the air of the southern spring. They had settled themselves for a couple of months in the queer hotel, which was once a monastery, perched high up under the still higher overhanging rocks, far above the beach and the busy little town; and now, in the May afternoon, they sat side by side under the trellis of vines on the terraced walk, their faces turned southward, in the shade of the steep mountain behind them; the sea was blue at their feet, and quite still, but farther out the westerly breeze that swept past the Conca combed it to crisp roughness; then it was less blue to southward, and gradually it grew less real, till it lost colour and melted into a sky-haze that almost hid the southern mountains and the lizard-like head of the far Licosa.

A bit of coarse faded carpet lay upon the ground under the two ladies' feet, and the shady air had a soft green tinge in it from the young vine-leaves overhead. At first sight one would have said that both were delicate, if not ill. Both were fair, though in different degrees, and both were pale and quiet, and looked a little weary.

The young girl sat in the deep straw chair, hatless, with bare white hands that held her work. Her thick flaxen hair, straightly parted and smoothed away from its low growth on the forehead, half hid small fresh ears, unpierced. Long lashes, too white for beauty, cast very faint light shadows as she looked down; but when she raised the lids, the dark-blue eyes were bright, with wide pupils and a straight look, quick to fasten, slow to let go, never yet quite softened, and yet never mannishly hard. But, in its own way, perhaps, there is no look so hard as the look of maiden innocence can be. There can even be something terrible in its unconscious stare. There is the spirit of God's own fearful directness in it. Half quibbling with words perhaps, but surely with half truth, one might say that youth "is," while all else "has been"; and that youth alone possesses the present, too innocent to know it all, yet too selfish even to doubt of what is its own — too sure of itself to doubt anything, to fear anything, or even truly to pray for anything. There is no

equality and no community in virtue; it is only
original sin that makes us all equal and human.
Old Lucifer, fallen, crushed, and damned, knows
the worth of forgiveness — not young Michael,
flintily hard and monumentally upright in his
steel coat, a terror to the devil himself. And
youth can have something of that archangelic
rigidity. Youth is not yet quite human.

But there was much in Clare Bowring's face
which told that she was to be quite human some
day. The lower features were not more than
strong enough — the curved lips would be fuller
before long, the small nostrils, the gentle chin,
were a little sharper than was natural, now, from
illness, but round in outline and not over promi-
nent; and the slender throat was very delicate
and feminine. Only in the dark-blue eyes there
was still that unabashed, quick glance and long-
abiding straightness, and innocent hardness, and
the unconscious selfishness of the uncontami-
nated.

Standing on her feet, she would have seemed
rather tall than short, though really but of average height. Seated, she looked tall, and her
glance was a little downward to most people's
eyes. Just now she was too thin, and seemed
taller than she was. But the fresh light was
already in the young white skin, and there was
a soft colour in the lobes of the little ears, as

the white leaves of daisies sometimes blush all round their tips.

The nervous white hands held the little bag lightly, and twined it and sewed it deftly, for Clare was clever with her fingers. Possibly they looked even a little whiter than they were, by contrast with the dark stuff of her dress, and illness had made them shrink at the lower part, robbing them of their natural strength, though not of their grace. There is a sort of refinement, not of taste, nor of talent, but of feeling and thought, and it shows itself in the hands of those who have it, more than in any feature of the face, in a sort of very true proportion between the hand and its fingers, between each finger and its joints, each joint and each nail; a something which says that such a hand could not do anything ignoble, could not take meanly, nor strike cowardly, nor press falsely; a quality of skin neither rough and coarse, nor over smooth like satin, but cool and pleasant to the touch as fine silk that is closely woven. The fingers of such hands are very straight and very elastic, but not supple like young snakes, as some fingers are, and the cushion of the hand is not over full nor heavy, nor yet shrunken and undeveloped as in the wasted hands of old Asiatic races.

In outward appearance there was that sort of inherited likeness between mother and daughter which is apt to strike strangers more than persons of the same family. Mrs. Bowring had been beautiful in her youth — far more beautiful than Clare — but her face had been weaker, in spite of the regularity of the features and their faultless proportion. Life had given them an acquired strength, but not of the lovely kind, and the complexion was faded, and the hair had darkened, and the eyes had paled. Some faces are beautified by suffering. Mrs. Bowring's face was not of that class. It was as though a thin, hard mask had been formed and closely moulded upon it, as the action of the sea overlays some sorts of soft rock with a surface thin as paper but as hard as granite. In spite of the hardness, the features were not really strong. There was refinement in them, however, of the same kind which the daughter had, and as much, though less pleasing. A fern — a spray of maiden's-hair — loses much of its beauty but none of its refinement when petrified in limestone or made fossil in coal.

As they sat there, side by side, mother and daughter, where they had sat every day for a week or more, they had very little to say. They had exhausted the recapitulation of Clare's illness, during the first days of her convalescence. It was not the first time that they had been in Amalfi, and they had enumerated its beauties to

each other, and renewed their acquaintance with
it from a distance, looking down from the terrace upon the low-lying town, and the beach
and the painted boats, and the little crowd that
swarmed out now and then like ants, very busy
and very much in a hurry, running hither and
thither, disappearing presently as by magic, and
leaving the shore to the sun and the sea.   The
two had spoken of a little excursion to Ravello,
and they meant to go thither as soon as they
should be strong enough; but that was not yet.
And meanwhile they lived through the quiet
days, morning, meal times, evening, bed time,
and round again, through the little hotel's pro-
gramme of possibility; eating what was offered
them, but feasting royally on air and sunshine
and spring sweetness; moistening their lips
in strange southern wines, but drinking deep
draughts of the rich southern air-life; watching the people of all sorts and of many conditions, who came and stayed a day and went
away again, but social only in each other's lives,
and even that by sympathy rather than in speech.
A corner of life's show was before them, and
they kept their places on the vine-sheltered terrace and looked on.   But it seemed as though
nothing could ever possibly happen there to
affect the direction of their own quietly moving
existence.

Seeing that her daughter did not say anything in answer to the remark about the past being written in a foreign language, Mrs. Bowring looked at the distant sky-haze thoughtfully for a few moments, then opened her book again where her thin forefinger had kept the place, and began to read. There was no disappointment in her face at not being understood, for she had spoken almost to herself and had expected no reply. No change of expression softened or accentuated the quiet hardness which overspread her naturally gentle face. But the thought was evidently still present in her mind, for her attention did not fix itself upon her book, and presently she looked at her daughter, as the latter bent her head over the little bag she was making.

The young girl felt her mother's eyes upon her, looked up herself, and smiled faintly, almost mechanically, as before. It was a sort of habit they both had — a way of acknowledging one another's presence in the world. But this time it seemed to Clare that there was a question in the look, and after she had smiled she spoke.

" No," she said, " I don't understand how anybody can forget the past. It seems to me that I shall always remember why I did things, said things, and thought things. I should, if I lived a hundred years, I'm quite sure."

"Perhaps you have a better memory than I," answered Mrs. Bowring. "But I don't think it is exactly a question of memory either. I can remember what I said, and did, and thought, well — twenty years ago. But it seems to me very strange that I should have thought, and spoken, and acted, just as I did. After all isn't it natural? They tell us that our bodies are quite changed in less time than that." .

"Yes — but the soul does not change," said Clare with conviction.

"The soul — "

Mrs. Bowring repeated the word, but said nothing more, and her still, blue eyes wandered from her daughter's face and again fixed themselves on an imaginary point of the far southern distance.

"At least," said Clare, "I was always taught so."

She smiled again, rather coldly, as though admitting that such teaching might not be infallible after all.

"It is best to believe it," said her mother quietly, but in a colourless voice. "Besides," she added, with a change of tone, "I do believe it, you know. One is always the same, in the main things. It is the point of view that changes. The best picture in the world does not look the same in every light, does it?"

"No, I suppose not. You may like it in one light and not in another, and in one place and not in another."

"Or at one time of life, and not at another," added Mrs. Bowring, thoughtfully.

"I can't imagine that." Clare paused a moment. "Of course you are thinking of people," she continued presently, with a little more animation. "One always means people, when one talks in that way. And that is what I cannot quite understand. It seems to me that if I liked people once I should always like them."

Her mother looked at her.

"Yes — perhaps you would," she said, and she relapsed into silence.

Clare's colour did not change. No particular person was in her thoughts, and she had, as it were, given her own general and inexperienced opinion of her own character, quite honestly and without affectation.

"I don't know which are the happier," said Mrs. Bowring at last, "the people who change, or the people who can't."

"You mean faithful or unfaithful people, I suppose," observed the young girl with grave innocence.

A very slight flush rose in Mrs. Bowring's thin cheeks, and the quiet eyes grew suddenly hard, but Clare was busy with her work again and did not see.

" Those are big words," said the older woman in a low voice.

" Well — yes — of course ! " answered Clare. " So they ought to be ! It is always the main question, isn't it ? Whether you can trust a person or not, I mean."

" That is one question. The other is, whether the person deserves to be trusted."

" Oh — it's the same thing ! "

" Not exactly."

" You know what I mean, mother. Besides, I don't believe that any one who can't trust is really to be trusted. Do you ? "

" My dear Clare ! " exclaimed Mrs. Bowring. " You can't put life into a nutshell, like that ! "

" No. I suppose not, though if a thing is true at all it must be always true."

" Saving exceptions."

" Are there any exceptions to truth ? " asked Clare incredulously. " Truth isn't grammar — nor the British Constitution."

" No. But then, we don't know everything. What we call truth is what we know. It is only what we know. All that we don't know, but which is, is true, too — especially, all that we don't know about people with whom we have to live."

"Oh — if people have secrets!" The young girl laughed idly. "But you and I, for instance, mother — we have no secrets from each other, have we? Well? Why should any two people who love each other have secrets? And if they have none, why, then, they know all that there is to be known about one another, and each trusts the other, and has a right to be trusted, because everything is known — and everything is the whole truth. It seems to me that is simple enough, isn't it?"

Mrs. Bowring laughed in her turn. It was rather a hard little laugh, but Clare was used to the sound of it, and joined in it, feeling that she had vanquished her mother in argument, and settled one of the most important questions of life for ever.

"What a pretty steamer!" exclaimed Mrs. Bowring suddenly.

"It's a yacht," said Clare after a moment. "The flag is English, too. I can see it distinctly."

She laid down her work, and her mother closed her book upon her forefinger again, and they watched the graceful white vessel as she glided slowly in from the Conca, which she had rounded while they had been talking.

"It's very big, for a yacht," observed Mrs. Bowring. "They are coming here."

c

"They have probably come round from Naples to spend a day," said Clare. "We are sure to have them up here. What a nuisance!"

"Yes. Everybody comes up here who comes to Amalfi at all. I hope they won't stay long."

"There is no fear of that," answered Clare. "I heard those people saying the other day that this is not a place where a vessel can lie any length of time. You know how the sea sometimes breaks on the beach."

Mrs. Bowring and her daughter desired of all things to be quiet. The visitors who came, stayed a few days at the hotel, and went away again, were as a rule tourists or semi-invalids in search of a climate, and anything but noisy. But people coming in a smart English yacht would probably be society people, and as such Mrs. Bowring wished that they would keep away. They would behave as though the place belonged to them, so long as they remained; they would get all the attention of the proprietor and of the servants for the time being; and they would make everybody feel shabby and poor.

The Bowrings were poor, indeed, but they were not shabby. It was perhaps because they were well aware that nobody could mistake them for average tourists that they resented the coming of a party which belonged to what is called society. Mrs. Bowring had a strong aversion to making new acquaintances, and even disliked being thrown into the proximity of people who might know friends of hers, who might have heard of her, and who might talk about her and her daughter. Clare said that her mother's shyness in this respect was almost morbid; but she had unconsciously caught a little of it herself, and, like her mother, she was often quite uselessly on her guard against strangers, of the kind whom she might possibly be called upon to know, though she was perfectly affable and at her ease with those whom she looked upon as undoubtedly her social inferiors.

They were not mistaken in their prediction that the party from the yacht would come up to the Cappuccini. Half an hour after the yacht had dropped anchor the terrace was invaded. They came up in twos and threes, nearly a dozen of them, men and women, smart-looking people with healthy, sun-burnt faces, voices loud from the sea as voices become on a long voyage — or else very low indeed. By contrast with the frequenters of Amalfi they all seemed to wear overpoweringly good clothes and perfectly new hats and caps, and their russet shoes were resplendent. They moved as though everything belonged to them, from the wild crests of the hills above to the calm blue water below, and the hotel servants did their best to foster the agreeable illusion. They all wanted chairs, and tables, and things to drink, and fruit. One very fair little lady with hard, restless eyes, and clad in white serge, insisted upon having grapes, and no one could convince her that grapes were not ripe in May.

" It's quite absurd!" she objected. " Of course they're ripe ! We had the most beautiful grapes at breakfast at Leo Cairngorm's the other day, so of course they must have them here. Brook! Do tell the man not to be absurd!"

"Man!" said the member of the party she had last addressed. " Do not þe absurd!"

" Sì, Signore," replied the black-whiskered Amalfitan servant with alacrity.

" You see!" cried the little lady triumphantly. " I told you so! You must insist with these people. You can always get what you want. Brook, where's my fan?"

She settled upon a straw chair — like a white butterfly. The others walked on towards the end of the terrace, but the young man whom she called Brook stood beside her, slowly lighting a cigarette, not five paces from Mrs. Bowring and Clare.

" I'm sure I don't know where your fan is," he said, with a short laugh, as he threw the end of the match over the wall.

"Well then, look for it!" she answered, rather sharply. "I'm awfully hot, and I want it."

He glanced at her before he spoke again.

"I don't know where it is," he said quietly, but there was a shade of annoyance in his face.

"I gave it to you just as we were getting into the boat," answered the lady in white. "Do you mean to say that you left it on board?"

"I think you must be mistaken," said the young man. "You must have given it to somebody else."

"It isn't likely that I should mistake you for any one else — especially to-day."

"Well — I haven't got it. I'll get you one in the hotel, if you'll have patience for a moment."

He turned and strode along the terrace towards the house. Clare Bowring had been watching the two, and she looked after the man as he moved rapidly away. He walked well, for he was a singularly well-made young fellow, who looked as though he were master of every inch of himself. She had liked his brown face and bright blue eyes, too, and somehow she resented the way in which the little lady ordered him about. She looked round and saw that her mother was watching him too. Then, as he disappeared, they both looked at the lady. She too had followed him with her eyes, and as she

turned her face sideways to the Bowrings Clare
thought that she was biting her lip, as though
something annoyed her or hurt her. She kept
her eyes on the door. Presently the young man
reappeared, bearing a palm-leaf fan in his hand
and blowing a cloud of cigarette smoke into the
air. Instantly the lady smiled, and the smile
brightened as he came near.

" Thank you — dear," she said as he gave her
the fan.

The last word was spoken in a lower tone, and
could certainly not have been heard by the other
members of the party, but it reached Clare's ears,
where she sat.

"Not at all," answered the young man
quietly.

But as he spoke he glanced quickly about
him, and his eyes met Clare's. She fancied
that she saw a look of startled annoyance
in them, and he coloured a little under his tan.
He had a very manly face, square and strong.
He bent down a little and said something in
a low voice. The lady in white half turned her
head, impatiently, but did not look quite round.
Clare saw, however, that her expression had
changed again, and that the smile was gone.

" If I don't care, why should you ? " were the
next words Clare heard, spoken impatiently and
petulantly.

"Thank you — dear," she said as he gave her the fan. — *Page* 22.

The man who answered to the name of Brook said nothing, but sat down on the parapet of the terrace, looking out over his shoulder to seaward. A few seconds later he threw away his half-smoked cigarette.

"I like this place," said the lady in white, quite audibly. "I think I shall send on board for my things and stay here."

The young man started as though he had been struck, and faced her in silence. He could not help seeing Clare Bowring beyond her.

"I'm going indoors, mother," said the young girl, rising rather abruptly. "I'm sure it must be time for tea. Won't you come too?"

The young man did not answer his companion's remark, but turned his face away again and looked seaward, listening to the retreating footsteps of the two ladies.

On the threshold of the hotel Clare felt a strong desire to look back again and see whether he had moved, but she was ashamed of it and went in, holding her head high and looking straight before her.

CHAPTER II

THE people from the yacht belonged to that class of men and women whose uncertainty, or indifference, about the future leads them to take possession of all they can lay hands on in the present, with a view to squeezing the world like a lemon for such enjoyment as it may yield. So long as they tarried at the old hotel, it was their private property. The Bowrings were forgotten; the two English old maids had no existence; the Russian invalid got no more hot water for his tea; the plain but obstinately inquiring German family could get no more information; even the quiet young French couple — a honeymoon couple — sank into insignificance. The only protest came from an American, whose wife was ill and never appeared, and who staggered the landlord by asking what he would sell the whole place for on condition of vacating the premises before dinner.

"They will be gone before dinner," the proprietor answered.

But they did not go. When it was already late somebody saw the moon rise, almost full,

and suggested that the moonlight would be very
fine, and that it would be amusing to dine at
the hotel table and spend the evening on the
terrace and go on board late.

" I shall," said the little lady in white serge,
" whatever the rest of you do. Brook! Send
somebody on board to get a lot of cloaks and
shawls and things. I am sure it is going to be
cold. Don't go away! I want you to take me
for a walk before dinner, so as to be nice and
hungry, you know."

For some reason or other, several of the party
laughed, and from their tone one might have
guessed that they were in the habit of laughing,
or were expected to laugh, at the lady's speeches.
And every one agreed that it would be much
nicer to spend the evening on the terrace, and
that it was a pity that they could not dine out
of doors because it would be far too cool. Then
the lady in white and the man called Brook
began to walk furiously up and down in the
fading light, while the lady talked very fast in
a low voice, except when she was passing within
earshot of some of the others, and the man
looked straight before him, answering occasionally in monosyllables.

Then there was more confusion in the hotel,
and the Russian invalid expressed his opinion
to the two English old maids, with whom he

fraternised, that dinner would be an hour late, thanks to their compatriots. But they assumed an expression appropriate when speaking of the peerage, and whispered that the yacht must belong to the Duke of Orkney, who, they had read, was cruising in the Mediterranean, and that the Duke was probably the big man in grey clothes who had a gold cigarette case. But in all this they were quite mistaken. And their repeated examinations of the hotel register were altogether fruitless, because none of the party had written their names in it. The old maids, however, were quite happy and resigned to waiting for their dinner. They presently retired to attempt for themselves what stingy nature had refused to do for them in the way of adornment, for the dinner was undoubtedly to be an occasion of state, and their eyes were to see the glory of a lord.

The party sat together at one end of the table, which extended the whole length of the high and narrow vaulted hall, while the guests staying in the hotel filled the opposite half. Most of the guests were more subdued than usual, and the party from the yacht seemed noisy by contrast. The old maids strained their ears to catch a name here and there. Clare and her mother talked little. The Russian invalid put up a single eyeglass, looked long and curiously at each of the new comers in turn, and then did not vouchsafe them another glance. The German family criticised the food severely, and then got into a fierce discussion about Bismarck and the Pope, in the course of which they forgot the existence of their fellow-diners, but not of their dinner.

Clare could not help glancing once or twice at the couple that had attracted her attention, and she found herself wondering what their relation to each other could be, and whether they were engaged to be married. Somebody called the lady in white " Mrs. Crosby." Then somebody else called her " Lady Fan " — which was very confusing. " Brook " never called her anything. Clare saw him fill his glass and look at Lady Fan very hard before he drank, and then Lady Fan did the same thing. Nevertheless they seemed to be perpetually quarrelling over little things. When Brook was tired of being bullied, he calmly ignored his companion, turned from her, and talked in a low tone to a dark woman who had been a beauty and was the most thoroughly well-dressed of the extremely well-dressed party. Lady Fan bit her lip for a moment, and then said something at which all the others laughed — except Brook and the advanced beauty, who continued to talk in undertones.

To Clare's mind there was about them all, except Brook, a little dash of something which was not "quite, quite," as the world would have expressed it. In her opinion Lady Fan was distinctly disagreeable, whoever she might be — as distinctly so as Brook was the contrary. And somehow the girl could not help resenting the woman's way of treating him. It offended her oddly and jarred upon her good taste, as something to which she was not at all accustomed in her surroundings. Lady Fan was very exquisite in her outward ways, and her speech was of the proper smartness. Yet everything she did and said was intensely unpleasant to Clare.

The Bowrings and the regular guests finished their dinner before the yachting party, and rose almost in a body, with a clattering of their light chairs on the tiled floor. Only the English old maids kept their places a little longer than the rest, and took some more filberts and half a glass of white wine, each. They could not keep their eyes from the party at the other end of the table, and their faces grew a little redder as they sat there. Clare and her mother had to go round the long table to get out, being the last on their side, and they were also the last to reach the door. Again the young girl felt that strong desire to turn her

your pardon," he was saying, " you have dropped your
shawl." — *Page* 29.

head and look back at Brook and Lady Fan. She noticed it this time, as something she had never felt until that afternoon, but she would not yield to it. She walked on, looking straight at the back of her mother's head. Then she heard quick footsteps on the tiles behind her, and Brook's voice.

"I beg your pardon," he was saying, "you have dropped your shawl."

She turned quickly, and met his eyes as he stopped close to her, holding out the white chudder which had slipped to the floor unnoticed when she had risen from her seat. She took it mechanically and thanked him. Instinctively looking past him down the long hall, she saw that the little lady in white had turned in her seat and was watching her. Brook made a slight bow and was gone again in an instant. Then Clare followed her mother and went out.

"Let us go out behind the house," she said when they were in the broad corridor. "There will be moonlight there, and those people will monopolise the terrace when they have finished dinner."

At the western end of the old monastery there is a broad open space, between the buildings and the overhanging rocks, at the base of which there is a deep recess, almost amounting to a cave, in which stands a great black cross planted

in a pedestal of whitewashed masonry. A few
steps lead up to it. As the moon rose higher
the cross was in the shadow, while the platform
and the buildings were in the full light.

The two women ascended the steps and sat
down upon a stone seat.

"What a night!" exclaimed the young girl
softly.

Her mother silently bent her head, but neither
spoke again for some time. The moonlight before them was almost dazzling, and the air was
warm. Beyond the stone parapet, far below,
the tideless sea was silent and motionless under
the moon. A crooked fig-tree, still leafless,
though the little figs were already shaped on it,
cast its intricate shadow upon the platform.
Very far away, a boy was singing a slow minor
chant in a high voice. The peace was almost
disquieting — there was something intensely ex-
pectant in it, as though the night were in love,
and its heart beating.

Clare sat still, her hand upon her mother's
thin wrist, her lips just parted a little, her eyes
wide and filled with moon-dreams. She had
almost lost herself in unworded fancies when
her mother moved and spoke.

"I had quite forgotten a letter I was writing,"
she said. "I must finish it. Stay here, and I
will come back again presently."

She rose, and Clare watched her slim dark figure and the long black shadow that moved with it across the platform towards the open door of the hotel. But when it had disappeared the white fancies came flitting back through the silent light, and in the shade the young eyes fixed themselves quietly to meet the vision and see it all, and to keep it for ever if she could.

She did not know what it was that she saw, but it was beautiful, and what she felt was on a sudden as the realisation of something she had dimly desired in vain. Yet in itself it was nothing realised; it was perhaps only the certainty of longing for something all heart and no name, and it was happiness to long for it. For the first intuition of love is only an exquisite foretaste, a delight in itself, as far from the bitter hunger of love starving as a girl's faintness is from a cruel death. The light was dazzling, and yet it was full of gentle things that smiled, somehow, without faces. She was not very imaginative, perhaps, else the faces might have come too, and voices, and all, save the one reality which had as yet neither voice nor face, nor any name. It was all the something that love was to mean, somewhere, some day — the airy lace of a maiden life-dream, in which no figure was yet wrought amongst the fancy-threads that the May moon was weaving in the soft spring night.

There was no sadness in it, at all, for there was no memory, and without memory there can be no sadness, any more than there can be fear where there is no anticipation, far or near. Most happiness is really of the future, and most grief, if we would be honest, is of the past.

The young girl sat still and dreamed that the old world was as young as she, and that in its soft bosom there were exquisite sweetnesses untried, and soft yearnings for a beautiful unknown, and little pulses that could quicken with foretasted joy which only needed face and name to take angelic shape of present love. The world could not be old while she was young.

And she had her youth and knew it, and it was almost all she had. It seemed much to her, and she had no unsatisfiable craving for the world's stuff in which to attire it. In that, at least, her mother had been wise, teaching her to believe and to enjoy, rather than to doubt and criticise, and if there had been anything to hide from her it had been hidden, even beyond suspicion of its presence. Perhaps the armour of knowledge is of little worth until doubt has shaken the heart and weakened the joints, and broken the terrible steadfastness of perfect innocence in the eyes. Clare knew that she was young, she felt that the white dream was sweet, and she believed that the world's heart was clean and good. All good was natural and eternal, lofty and splendid as an archangel in the light. God had made evil as a background of shadows to show how good the light was. Every one could come and stand in the light if he chose, for the mere trouble of moving. It seemed so simple. She wondered why everybody could not see it as she did.

A flash of white in the white moonlight disturbed her meditations. Two people had come out of the door and were walking slowly across the platform side by side. They were not speaking, and their footsteps crushed the light gravel sharply as they came forward. Clare recognised Brook and Lady Fan. Seated in the shadow on one side of the great black cross and a little behind it, she could see their faces distinctly, but she had no idea that they were dazzled by the light and could not see her at all in her dark dress. She fancied that they were looking at her as they came on.

The shadow of the rock had crept forward upon the open space, while she had been dreaming. The two turned, just before they reached it, and then stood still, instead of walking back.

" Brook — " began Lady Fan, as though she were going to say something.

But she checked herself and looked up at him quickly, chilled already by his humour. Clare thought that the woman's voice shook a little, as she pronounced the name. Brook did not turn his head nor look down.

" Yes ? " he said, with a sort of interrogation. " What were you going to say? " he asked after a moment's pause.

She seemed to hesitate, for she did not answer at once. Then she glanced towards the hotel and looked down.

" You won't come back with us ? " she asked, at last, in a pleading voice.

" I can't," he answered. " You know I can't. I've got to wait for them here."

" Yes, I know. But they are not here yet. I don't believe they are coming for two or three days. You could perfectly well come on to Genoa with us, and get back by rail."

" No," said Brook quietly, " I can't."

" Would you, if you could ? " asked the lady in white, and her tone began to change again.

" What a question ! " he laughed drily.

" It is an odd question, isn't it, coming from me ? " Her voice grew hard, and she stopped. " Well — you know what it means," she added abruptly. " You may as well answer it and have it over. It is very easy to say you would not, if you could. I shall understand all the rest, and you will be saved the trouble of saying things — things which I should think you would find it rather hard to say."

"Couldn't you say them, instead?" he asked slowly, and looking at her for the first time. — *Page* 35.

"Couldn't you say them, instead?" he asked slowly, and looking at her for the first time. He spoke gravely and coldly.

"I!" There was indignation, real or well affected, in the tone.

"Yes, you," answered the man, with a shade less coldness, but as gravely as before. "You never loved me."

Lady Fan's small white face was turned to his instantly, and Clare could see the fierce, hurt expression in the eyes and about the quivering mouth. The young girl suddenly realised that she was accidentally overhearing something which was very serious to the two speakers. It flashed upon her that they had not seen her where she sat in the shadow, and she looked about her hastily in the hope of escaping unobserved. But that was impossible. There was no way of getting out of the recess of the rock where the cross stood, except by coming out into the light, and no way of reaching the hotel except by crossing the open platform.

Then she thought of coughing, to call attention to her presence. She would rise and come forward, and hurry across to the door. She felt that she ought to have come out of the shadows as soon as the pair had appeared, and that she had done wrong in sitting still. But then, she told herself with perfect justice that they were strangers, and that she could not possibly have foreseen that they had come there to quarrel.

They were strangers, and she did not even know their names. So far as they were concerned, and their feelings, it would be much more pleasant for them if they never suspected that any one had overheard them than if she were to appear in the midst of their conversation, having evidently been listening up to that point. It will be admitted that, being a woman, she had a choice; for she knew that if she had been in Lady Fan's place she should have preferred never to know that any one had heard her. She fancied what she should feel if any one should cough unexpectedly behind her when she had just been accused by the man she loved of not loving him at all. And of course the little lady in white loved Brook — she had called him "dear" that very afternoon. But that Brook did not love Lady Fan was as plain as possible.

There was certainly no mean curiosity in Clare to know the secrets of these strangers. But all the same, she would not have been a human girl, of any period in humanity's history, if she had not been profoundly interested in the fate of the woman before her. That afternoon she would have thought it far more probable that the woman should break the man's heart than

that she should break her own for him. But
now it looked otherwise. Clare thought there
was no mistaking the first tremor of the voice,
the look of the white face, and the indignation
of the tone afterwards. With a man, the question of revealing his presence as a third person
would have been a point of honour. In Clare's
case it was a question of delicacy and kindness
as from one woman to another.

Nevertheless, she hesitated, and she might
have come forward after all. Ten slow seconds
had passed since Brook had spoken. Then Lady
Fan's little figure shook, her face turned away,
and she tried to choke down one small bitter
sob, pressing her handkerchief desperately to
her lips.

" Oh, Brook ! " she cried, a moment later, and
her tiny teeth tore the edge of the handkerchief audibly in the stillness.

" It's not your fault," said the man, with
an attempt at gentleness in his voice. " I
couldn't blame you, if I were brute enough to
wish to."

" Blame me ! Oh, really — I think you're
mad, you know ! "

" Besides," continued the young man, philo-
sophically, " I think we ought to be glad, don't
you ? "

" Glad ? "

"Yes — that we are not going to break our hearts now that it's over."

Clare thought his tone horribly business-like and indifferent.

"Oh no! We sha'n't break our hearts any more! We are not children." Her voice was thin and bitter, with a crying laugh in it.

"Look here, Fan!" said Brook suddenly. "This is all nonsense. We agreed to play together, and we've played very nicely, and now you have to go home, and I have got to stay here, whether I like it or not. Let us be good friends and say good-bye, and if we meet again and have nothing better to do, we can play again if we please. But as for taking it in this tragical way — why, it isn't worth it."

The young girl crouching in the shadow felt as though she had been struck, and her heart went out with indignant sympathy to the little lady in white.

"Do you know? I think you are the most absolutely brutal, cynical creature I ever met!" There was anger in the voice, now, and something more — something which Clare could not understand.

"Well, I'm sorry," answered the man. "I don't mean to be brutal, I'm sure, and I don't think I'm cynical either. I look at things as they are, not as they ought to be. We are not angels, and the millennium hasn't come yet. I suppose it would be bad for us if it did, just now. But we used to be very good friends last year. I don't see why we shouldn't be again."

" Friends! Oh no ! "

Lady Fan turned from him and made a step or two alone, out through the moonlight, towards the house. Brook did not move. Perhaps he knew that she would come back, as indeed she did, stopping suddenly and turning round to face him again.

"Brook," she began more softly, "do you remember that evening up at the Acropolis — at sunset? Do you remember what you said?"

"Yes, I think I do."

"You said that if I could get free you would marry me."

"Yes." The man's tone had changed suddenly.

"Well — I believed you, that's all."

Brook stood quite still, and looked at her quietly. Some seconds passed before she spoke again.

"You did not mean it?" she asked sorrowfully.

. Still he said nothing.

"Because you know," she continued, her eyes fixed on his, " the position is not at all impossible. All things considered, I suppose I could have a divorce for the asking."

Clare started a little in the dark. She was beginning to guess something of the truth she could not understand. The man still said nothing, but he began to walk up and down slowly, with folded arms, along the edge of the shadow before Lady Fan as she stood still, following him with her eyes.

" You did not mean a word of what you said that afternoon? Not one word?" She spoke very slowly and distinctly.

He was silent still, pacing up and down before her. Suddenly, without a word, she turned from him and walked quickly away, towards the hotel. He started and stood still, looking after her — then he also made a step.

" Fan!" he called, in a tone she could hear, but she went on. " Mrs. Crosby!" he called again.

She stopped, turned, and waited. It was clear that Lady Fan was a nickname, Clare thought.

" Well?" she asked.

Clare clasped her hands together in her excitement, watching and listening, and holding her breath.

" Don't go like that!" exclaimed Brook, going forward and holding out one hand.

"Do you want me?" asked the lady in white, very gently, almost tenderly. Clare did not understand how any woman could have so little pride, but she pitied the little lady from her heart.

Brook went on till he came up with Lady Fan, who did not make a step to meet him. But just as he reached her she put out her hand to take his. Clare thought he was relenting, but she was mistaken. His voice came back to her clear and distinct, and it had a very gentle ring in it.

"Fan, dear," he said, "we have been very fond of each other in our careless way. But we have not loved each other. We may have thought that we did, for a moment, now and then. I shall always be fond of you, just in that way. I'll do anything for you. But I won't marry you, if you get a divorce. It would be utter folly. If I ever said I would, in so many words — well, I'm ashamed of it. You'll forgive me some day. One says things — sometimes — that one means for a minute, and then, afterwards, one doesn't mean them. But I mean what I am saying now."

He dropped her hand, and stood looking at her, and waiting for her to speak. Her face, as Clare saw it, from a distance now, looked whiter than ever. After an instant she turned from him with a quick movement, but not towards the hotel.

She walked slowly towards the stone parapet of the platform. As she went, Clare again saw her raise her handkerchief and press it to her lips, but she did not bend her head. She went and leaned on her elbows on the parapet, and her hands pulled nervously at the handkerchief as she looked down at the calm sea far below. Brook followed her slowly, but just as he was near, she, hearing his footsteps, turned and leaned back against the low wall.

"Give me a cigarette," she said in a hard voice. "I'm nervous—and I've got to face those people in a moment."

Clare started again in sheer surprise. She had expected tears, fainting, angry words, a passionate appeal — anything rather than what she heard. Brook produced a silver case which gleamed in the moonlight. Lady Fan took a cigarette, and her companion took another. He struck a match and held it up for her in the still air. The little flame cast its red glare into their faces. The young girl had good eyes, and as she watched them she saw the man's expression was grave and stern, a little sad, perhaps, but she fancied that there was the beginning of a scornful smile on the woman's lips. She understood less clearly then than ever what manner of human beings these two strangers might be.

For some moments they smoked in silence, the lady in white leaning back against the parapet, the man standing upright with one hand in his pocket, holding his cigarette in the other, and looking out to sea. Then Lady Fan stood up, too, and threw her cigarette over the wall.

" It's time to be going," she said, suddenly. " They'll be coming after us if we stay here."

But she did not move. Sideways she looked up into his face. Then she held out her hand.

" Good-bye, Brook," she said, quietly enough, as he took it.

" Good-bye," he murmured in a low voice, but distinctly.

Their hands stayed together after they had spoken, and still she looked up to him in the moonlight. Suddenly he bent down and kissed her on the forehead — in an odd, hasty way.

" I'm sorry, Fan, but it won't do," he said.

" Again!" she answered. " Once more, please!" And she held up her face.

He kissed her again, but less hastily, Clare thought, as she watched them. Then, without another word, they walked towards the hotel, side by side, close together, so that their hands almost touched. When they were not ten paces from the door, they stopped again and looked at each other.

At that moment Clare saw her mother's dark figure on the threshold. The pair must have heard her steps, for they separated a little and instantly went on, passing Mrs. Bowring quickly. Clare sat still in her place, waiting for her mother to come to her. She feared lest, if she moved, the two might come back for an instant, see her, and understand that they had been watched. Mrs. Bowring went forward a few steps.

" Clare ! " she called.

" Yes," answered the young girl softly. " Here I am."

" Oh — I could not see you at all," said her mother. " Come down into the moonlight."

The young girl descended the steps, and the two began to walk up and down together on the platform.

" Those were two of the people from the yacht that I met at the door," said Mrs. Bowring. " The lady in white serge, and that good-looking young man."

" Yes," Clare answered. " They were here some time. I don't think they saw me."

She had meant to tell her mother something of what had happened, in the hope of being told that she had done right in not revealing her presence. But on second thoughts she resolved to say nothing about it. To have told the story would have seemed like betraying a confidence, even though they were strangers to her.

"I could not help wondering about them this afternoon," said Mrs. Bowring. "She ordered him about in a most extraordinary way, as though he had been her servant. I thought it in very bad taste, to say the least of it. Of course I don't know anything about their relations, but it struck me that she wished to show him off, as her possession."

"Yes," answered Clare, thoughtfully. "I thought so too."

"Very foolish of her! No man will stand that sort of thing long. That isn't the way to treat a man in order to keep him."

"What is the best way?" asked the young girl idly, with a little laugh.

"Don't ask me!" answered Mrs. Bowring quickly, as they turned in their walk. "But I should think —" she added, a moment later, "I don't know — but I should think —" she hesitated.

"What?" inquired Clare, with some curiosity.

"Well, I was going to say, I should think that a man would wish to feel that he is holding, not that he is held. But then people are so different! One can never tell. At all events, it is foolish to wish to show everybody that you own a man, so to say."

Mrs. Bowring seemed to be considering the question, but she evidently found nothing more to say about it, and they walked up and down in silence for a long time, each occupied with her own thoughts. Then all at 'once there was a sound of many voices speaking English, and trying to give orders in Italian, and the words "Good-bye, Brook!" sounded several times above the rest. Little by little, all grew still again.

"They are gone at last," said Mrs. Bowring, with a sigh of relief.

CHAPTER III

CLARE BOWRING went to her room that night
feeling as though she had been at the theatre.
She could not get rid of the impression made
upon her by the scene she had witnessed, and
over and over again, as she lay awake, with the
moonbeams streaming into her room, she went
over all she had seen and heard on the platform.
It had, at least, been very like the theatre.
The broad, flat stage, the somewhat convention-
ally picturesque buildings, the strip of far-off
sea, as flat as a band of paint, the unnaturally
bright moonlight, the two chief figures going
through a love quarrel in the foreground, and
she herself calmly seated in the shadow, as in
the darkened amphitheatre, and looking on un-
seen and unnoticed.

But the two people had not talked at all as
people talked on the stage in any piece Clare
had ever seen. What would have been the
"points" in a play had all been left out, and
instead there had been abrupt pauses and awkward silences, and then, at what should have
been the supreme moment, the lady in white

47

had asked for a cigarette. And the two hasty little kisses that had a sort of perfunctory air, and the queer, jerky " good-byes," and the last stop near the door of the hotel — it all had an air of being very badly done. It could not have been a success on the stage, Clare thought.

And yet this was a bit of life, of the real, genuine life of two people who had been in love, and perhaps were in love still, though they might not know it. She had been present at what must, in her view, have been a great crisis in two lives. Such things, she thought, could not happen more than once in a lifetime — twice, perhaps. Her mother had been married twice, so Clare admitted a second possibility. But not more than that.

The situation, too, as she reviewed it, was nothing short of romantic. Here was a young man who had evidently been making love to a married woman, and who had made her believe that he loved her, and had made her love him too. Clare remembered the desperate little sob, and the handkerchief twice pressed to the pale lips. The woman was married, and yet she actually loved the man enough to think of divorcing her husband in order to marry him. Then, just when she was ready, he had turned and told her in the most heartless way that it had been all play, and that he would not marry her under any circumstances. It seemed monstrous to the innocent girl that they should even have spoken of marriage, until the divorce was accomplished. Then, of course, it would have been all right. Clare had been brought up with modern ideas about divorce in general, as being a fair and just thing in certain circumstances. She had learned that it could not be right to let an innocent woman suffer all her life because she had married a brute by mistake. Doubtless that was Lady Fan's case. But she should have got her divorce first, and then she might have talked of marriage afterwards. It was very wrong of her.

But Lady Fan's thoughtlessness — or wickedness, as Clare thought she ought to call it — sank into insignificance before the cynical heartlessness of the man. It was impossible ever to forget the cool way in which he had said she ought not to take it so tragically, because it was not worth it. Yet he had admitted that he had promised to marry her if she got a divorce. He had made love to her, there on the Acropolis, at sunset, as she had said. He even granted that he might have believed himself in earnest for a few moments. And now he told her that he was sorry, but that "it would not do." It had evidently been all his fault, for he had found nothing with which to reproach her. If there

E

had been anything, Clare thought, he would have
brought it up in self-defence. She could not suspect that he would almost rather have married
Lady Fan, and ruined his life, than have done
that. Innocence cannot even guess at sin's code
of honour — though sometimes it would be in
evil case without it. Brook had probably broken
Lady Fan's heart that night, thought the young
girl, though Lady Fan had said with such a bitter, crying laugh that they were not children
and that their hearts could not break.

And it all seemed very unreal, as she looked
back upon it. The situation was certainly romantic, but the words had been poor beyond her
imagination, and the actors had halted in their
parts, as at a first rehearsal.

Then Clare reflected that of course neither of
them had ever been in such a situation before,
and that, if they were not naturally eloquent, it
was not surprising that they should have expressed themselves in short, jerky sentences.
But that was only an excuse she made to herself
to account for the apparent unreality of it all.
She turned her cheek to a cool end of the pillow
and tried to go to sleep.

She tried to bring back the white dreams she
had dreamt when she had sat alone in the shadow
before the other two had come out to quarrel.
She did her best to bring back that vague, soft

joy of yearning for something beautiful and unknown. She tried to drop the silver veil of fancy-threads woven by the May moon between her and the world. But it would not come. Instead of it, she saw the flat platform, the man and woman standing in the unnatural brightness, and the woman's desperate little face when he had told her that she had never loved him. The dream was not white any more.

So that was life. That was reality. That was the way men treated women. She thought she began to understand what faithlessness and unfaithfulness meant. She had seen an unfaithful man, and had heard him telling the woman he had made love him that he never could love her any more. That was real life.

Clare's heart went out to the little lady in white. By this time she was alone in her cabin, and her pillow was wet with tears. Brook doubtless was calmly asleep, unless he were drinking or doing some of those vaguely wicked things which, in the imagination of very simple young girls, fill up the hours of fast men, and help sometimes to make those very men "interesting." But after what she had seen Clare felt that Brook could never interest her under imaginable circumstances. He was simply a "brute," as the lady in white had told him, and Clare wished that some woman could make him suffer

for his sins and expiate the misdeeds which had
made that little face so desperate and that short
laugh so bitter.

She wished, though she hardly knew it, that
she had done anything rather than have sat
there in the shadow, all through the scene. She
had lost something that night which it would be
hard indeed to find again. There was a big
jagged rent in the drop-curtain of illusions before
her life-stage, and through it she saw things
that troubled her and would not be forgotten.

She had no memory of her own of which the
vivid brightness or the intimate sadness could
diminish the force of this new impression. Possibly, she was of the kind that do not easily fall
in love, for she had met during the past two
years more than one man whom many a girl of
her age and bringing up might have fancied.
Some of them might have fallen in love with
her, if she had allowed them, or if she had felt
the least spark of interest in them and had
shown it. But she had not. Her manner was
cold and over-dignified for her years, and she
had very little vanity together with much pride
—too much of the latter, perhaps, to be ever
what is called popular. For "popular" persons
are generally those who wish to be such; and
pride and the love of popularity are at opposite
poles of the character-world. Proud characters

set love high and their own love higher, while a
vain woman will risk her heart for a compliment, and her reputation for the sake of having
a lion in her leash, if only for a day. Clare
Bowring had not yet been near to loving, and
she had nothing of her own to contrast with this
experience in which she had been a mere spec-
tator. It at once took the aspect of a generality.
This man and this woman were probably not
unlike most men and women, if the truth were
known, she thought. And she had seen the real
truth, as few people could ever have seen it —
the supreme crisis of a love-affair going on before
her very eyes, in her hearing, at her feet, the
actors having no suspicion of her presence. It
was, perhaps, the certainty that she could not
misinterpret it all which most disgusted her, and
wounded something in her which she had never
defined, but which was really a sort of belief
that love must always carry with it something
beautiful, whether joyous, or tender, or tragic.
Of that, there had been nothing in what she had
seen. Only the woman's face came back to her,
and hurt her, and she felt her own heart go out
to poor Lady Fan, while it hardened against
Brook with an exaggerated hatred, as though
he had insulted and injured all living women.

It was probable that she was to see this man
during several days to come. The idea struck

.

her when she was almost asleep, and it waked
her again, with a start. It was quite certain
that he had stayed behind, when the others had
gone down to the yacht, for she had heard the
voices calling out " Good-bye, Brook ! " Besides
he had said repeatedly to the lady in white that
he must stay. He was expecting his people. It
was quite certain that Clare must see him during
the next day or two. It was not impossible that
he might try to make her mother's acquaintance
and her own. The idea was intensely disagreeable to her. In the first place, she hated him
beforehand for what he had done, and, secondly,
she had once heard his secret. It was one thing,
so long as he was a total stranger. It would be
quite another, if she should come to know him.
She had a vague thought of pretending to be ill,
and staying in her room as long as he remained
in the place. But in that case she should have
to explain matters to her mother. She should
not like to do that. The thought of the difficulty disturbed her a little while longer. Then,
at last, she fell asleep, tired with what she had
felt, and seen, and heard.

The yacht sailed before daybreak, and in the
morning the little hotel had returned to its nor-
mal state of peace. The early sun blazed upon
the white walls above, and upon the half-moon
beach below, and shot straight into the recess in

She was like a thin, fair angel, standing there. — *Page* 55.

the rocks where Clare had sat by the old black
cross in the dark. The level beams ran through
her room, too, for it faced south-east, looking
across the gulf; and when she went to the window and stood in the sunshine, her flaxen hair
looked almost white, and the good southern
warmth brought soft colour to the northern
girl's cheeks. She was like a thin, fair angel,
standing there on the high balcony, looking to
seaward in the calm air. That, at least, was
what a fisherman from Praiano thought, as he
turned his hawk-eyes upwards, standing to his
oars and paddling slowly along, topheavy in his
tiny boat. But no native of Amalfi ever mistook
a foreigner for an angel.

Everything was quiet and peaceful again, and
there seemed to be neither trace nor memory of
the preceding day's invasion. The English old
maids were early at their window, and saw with
disappointment that the yacht was gone. They
were never to know whether the big man with
the gold cigarette case had been the Duke of
Orkney or not. But order was restored, and
they got their tea and toast without difficulty.
The Russian invalid was slicing a lemon into his
cup on the vine-sheltered terrace, and the German family, having slept on the question of the
Pope and Bismarck, were ruddy with morning
energy, and were making an early start for a

place in the hills where the Professor had heard
that there was an inscription of the ninth
century.

The young girl stood still on her balcony,
happily dazed for a few moments by the strong
sunshine and the clear air. It is probably the
sensation enjoyed for hours together by a dog
basking in the sun, but with most human beings
it does not last long — the sun is soon too hot
for the head, or too bright for the eyes, or there
is a draught, or the flies disturb one. Man is
not capable of as much physical enjoyment as
the other animals, though perhaps his enjoyment
is keener during the first moments. Then comes
thought, restlessness, discontent, change, effort,
and progress, and the history of man's superior-
ity is the journal of his pain.

For a little while, Clare stood blinking in the
sunshine, smitten into a pleasant semi-conscious-
ness by the strong nature around her. Then she
thought of Brook and the lady in white, and of
all she had been a witness of in the evening, and
the colour of things changed a little, and she
turned away and went between the little white
and red curtains into her room again. Life was
certainly not the same since she had heard and
seen what a man and a woman could say and be.
There were certain new impressions, where there
had been no impression at all, but only a maiden

readiness to receive the beautiful. What had come was not beautiful, by any means, and the thought of it darkened the air a little, so that the day was not to be what it might have been. She realised how she was affected, and grew impatient with herself. After all, it would be the easiest thing in the world to avoid the man, even if he stayed some time. Her mother was not much given to making acquaintance with strangers.

And it would have been easy enough, if the man himself had taken the same view. He, however, had watched the Bowrings on the preceding evening, and had made up his mind that they were "human beings," as he put it; that is to say, that they belonged to his own class, whereas none of the people at the upper end of the table had any claim to be counted with the social blessed. He was young, and though he knew how to amuse himself alone, and had all manner of manly tastes and inclinations, he preferred pleasant society to solitude, and his experience told him that the society of the Bowrings would in all probability be pleasant. He therefore determined that he would try to know them at once, and the determination had already been formed in his mind when he had run after Clare to give her the shawl she had dropped.

He got up rather late, and promptly marched out upon the terrace under the vines, smoking a briar-root pipe with that solemn air whereby the Englishman abroad proclaims to the world that he owns the scenery. There is something almost phenomenal about an Englishman's solid self-satisfaction when he is alone with his pipe. Every nation has its own way of smoking. There is a hasty and vicious manner about the Frenchman's little cigarette of pungent black tobacco; the Italian dreams over his rat-tail cigar; the American either eats half of his Havana while he smokes the other, or else he takes a frivolous delight in smoking delicately and keeping the white ash whole to the end; the German surrounds himself with a cloud, and, god-like, meditates within it; there is a sacrificial air about the Asiatic's narghileh, as the thin spire rises steadily and spreads above his head; but the Englishman's short briar-root pipe has a powerful individuality of its own. Its simplicity is Gothic, its solidity is of the Stone Age, he smokes it in the face of the higher civilisation, and it is the badge of the conqueror. A man who asserts that he has a right to smoke a pipe anywhere, practically asserts that he has a right to everything. And it will be admitted that Englishmen get a good deal.

Moreover, as soon as the Englishman has

finished smoking he generally goes and does something else. Brook knocked the ashes out of his pipe, and immediately went in search of the head waiter, to whom he explained with some difficulty that he wished to be placed next to the two ladies who sat last on the side away from the staircase at the public table. The waiter tried to explain that the two ladies, though they had been some time in the hotel, insisted upon being always last on that side because there was more air. But Brook was firm, and he strengthened his argument with coin, and got what he wanted. He also made the waiter point out to him the Bowrings' name on the board which held the names of the guests. Then he asked the way to Ravello, turned up his trousers round his ankles, and marched off at a swinging pace down the steep descent towards the beach, which he had to cross before climbing the hill to the old town. Nothing in his outward manner or appearance betrayed that he had been through a rather serious crisis on the preceding evening.

That was what struck Clare Bowring when, to her dismay, he sat down beside her at the midday meal. She could not help glancing at him as he took his seat. His eyes were bright, his face, browned by the sun, was fresh and rested. There was not a line of care or thought

on his forehead. The young girl felt that she
was flushing with anger. He saw her colour,
and took it for a sign of shyness. He made a
sort of apologetic movement of the head and
shoulders towards her which was not exactly a
bow — for to an Englishman's mind a bow is
almost a familiarity — but which expressed a
kind of vague desire not to cause any incon-
venience.

The colour deepened a little in Clare's face,
and then disappeared. She found something to
say to her mother, on her other side, which it
would hardly have been worth while to say at
all under ordinary circumstances. Mrs. Bowring
had glanced at the man while he was taking his
seat, and her eyebrows had contracted a little.
Later she looked furtively past her daughter at
his profile, and then stared a long time at her
plate. As for him, he began to eat with conscious strength, as healthy young men do, but he
watched his opportunity for doing or saying anything which might lead to a first acquaintance.

To tell the truth, however, he was in no
hurry. He knew how to make himself comfortable, and it was an important element in his
comfort to be seated next to the only persons in
the place with whom he should care to associate.
That point being gained, he was willing to wait
for whatever was to come afterwards. He did

not expect in any case to gain more than the chance of a little pleasant conversation, and he was not troubled by any youthful desire to shine in the eyes of the fair girl beside whom he found himself, beyond the natural wish to appear well before women in general, which modifies the conduct of all natural and manly young men when women are present at all.

As the meal proceeded, however, he was surprised to find that no opportunity presented itself for exchanging a word with his neighbour. He had so often found it impossible to avoid speaking with strangers at a public table that he had taken the probability of some little incident for granted, and caught himself glancing surreptitiously at Clare's plate to see whether there were nothing wanting which he might offer her. But he could not think of anything. The fried sardines were succeeded by the regulation braised beef with the gluey brown sauce which grows in most foreign hotels. That, in its turn, was followed by some curiously dry slices of spongecake, each bearing a bit of pink and white sugar frosting, and accompanied by fresh orange marmalade, which Brook thought very good, but which Clare refused. And then there was fruit — beautiful oranges, uncanny apples, and walnuts — and the young man foresaw the near end of the meal, and wished that something would happen. But still nothing happened at all.

He watched Clare's hands as she prepared an orange in the Italian fashion, taking off the peel at one end, then passing the knife twice completely round at right angles, and finally stripping the peel away in four neat pieces. The hands were beautiful in their way, too thin, perhaps, and almost too white from recent illness, but straight and elastic, with little blue veins at the sides of the finger-joints and exquisite nails that were naturally polished. The girl was clever with her fingers, she could not help seeing that her neighbour was watching her, and she peeled the orange with unusual skill and care. It was a good one, too, and the peel separated easily from the deep yellow fruit.

" How awfully jolly ! " exclaimed the young man, unconsciously, in genuine admiration.

He was startled by the sound of his own voice, for he had not meant to speak, and the blood rushed to his sunburnt face. Clare's eyes flashed upon him in a glance of surprise, and the colour rose in her cheeks also. She was evidently not pleased, and he felt that he had been guilty of a breach of English propriety. When an Englishman does a tactless thing he generally hastens to make it worse, becomes suddenly shy, and flounders.

He watched Clare's hands as she prepared an orange in the Italian
fashion. — *Page 62.*

"I — I beg your pardon," stammered Brook. "I really didn't mean to speak — that is — you did it so awfully well, you know!"

"It's the Italian way," Clare answered, beginning to quarter the orange.

She felt that she could not exactly be silent after he had apologised for admiring her skill. But she remembered that she had felt some vanity in what she had been doing, and had done it with some unnecessary ostentation. She hoped that he would not say anything more, for the sound of his voice reminded her of what she had heard him say to the lady in white, and she hated him with all her heart.

But the young man was encouraged by her sufficiently gracious answer, and was already glad of what he had done.

"Do all Italians do it that way?" he asked boldly.

"Generally," answered the young girl, and she began to eat the orange.

Brook took another from the dish before him.

"Let me see," he said, turning it round and round. "You cut a slice off one end." He began to cut the peel.

"Not too deep," said Clare, "or you will cut into the fruit."

"Oh — thanks, awfully. Yes, I see. This way?"

He took the end off, and looked at her for
approval. She nodded gravely, and then turned
away her eyes. He made the two cuts round
the peel, crosswise, and looked to her again, but
she affected not to see him.

"Oh — might I ask you —" he began. She
looked at his orange again, without a smile.
"Please don't think me too dreadfully rude,"
he said. "But it was so pretty, and I'm tremendously anxious to learn. Was it this way?"

His fingers teased the peel, and it began to
come off. He raised his eyes with another look
of inquiry.

"Yes. That's all right," said Clare calmly.

She was going to look away again, when she
reflected that since he was so pertinacious it
would be better to see the operation finished
once for all. Then she and her mother would
get up and go away, as they had finished. But
he wished to push his advantage.

"And now what does one do?" he asked, for
the sake of saying something.

"One eats it," answered Clare, half impatiently.

He stared at her a moment and then broke
into a laugh, and Clare, very much to her own
surprise and annoyance, laughed too, in spite of
herself. That broke the ice. When two people
have laughed together over something one of

them has said, there is no denying the acquaintance.

" It was really awfully kind of you ! " he exclaimed, his eyes still laughing. " It was horridly rude of me to say anything at all, but I
really couldn't help it. If I could get anybody
to introduce me, so that I could apologise properly, I would, you know, but in this place — "

He looked towards the German family and
the English old maids, in a helpless sort of way,
and then laughed again.

" I don't think it's necessary," said Clare,
rather coldly.

" No — I suppose not," he answered, growing
graver at once. " And I think it is allowed —
isn't it ? — to speak to one's neighbour at a table
d'hôte, you know. Not but what it was awfully
rude of me, all the same," he added hastily.

" Oh no. Not at all."

Clare stared at the wall opposite and leaned
back in her chair.

" Oh ! thanks awfully ! I was afraid you
might think so, you know."

Mrs. Bowring leaned forward as her daughter leaned back. Seeing that the latter had
fallen into conversation with the stranger, she
was too much a woman of the world not to
speak to him at once in order to avoid any
awkwardness when they next met, for he could

F

not possibly have spoken first to her across the young girl.

"Is it your first visit to Amalfi?" she inquired, with as much originality as is common in such cases.

Brook leaned forward too, and looked over at the elder woman.

"Yes," he answered, "I was with a party, and they dropped me here last night. I was to meet my people here, but they haven't turned up yet, so I'm seeing the sights. I went up to Ravello this morning — you know, that place on the hill. There's an awfully good view from there, isn't there?"

Clare thought his fluency developed very quickly when he spoke to her mother. As he leaned forward she could not help seeing his face, and she looked at him closely, for the first time, and with some curiosity. He was handsome, and had a wonderfully frank and good-humoured expression. He was not in the least a "beauty" man — she thought he might be a soldier or a sailor, and a very good specimen of either. Furthermore, he was undoubtedly a gentleman, so far as a man is to be judged by his outward manner and appearance. In her heart she had already set him down as little short of a villain. The discrepancy between his looks and what she thought of him disturbed her. It was

unpleasant to feel that a man who had acted as
he had acted last night could look as fresh, and
innocent, and unconcerned as he looked to-day.
It was disagreeable to have him at her elbow.
Either he had never cared a straw for poor Lady
Fan, and in that case he had almost broken her
heart out of sheer mischief and love of selfish
amusement, or else, if he had cared for her at all,
he was a pitiably fickle and faithless creature —
something much more despicable in the eyes of
most women than the most heartless cynic. One
or the other he must be, thought Clare. In either
case he was bad, because Lady Fan was married,
and it was wicked to make love to married
women. There was a directness about Clare's
view which would either have made the man
laugh or would have hurt him rather badly.
She wondered what sort of expression would
come over his handsome face if she were suddenly to tell him what she knew. The idea
took her by surprise, and she smiled to herself
as she thought of it.

Yet she could not help glancing at him again
and again, as he talked across her with her
mother, making very commonplace remarks
about the beauty of the place. Very much in
spite of herself, she wished to know him better,
though she already hated him. His face attracted
her strangely, and his voice was pleasant, close

to her ear. He had not in the least the look of
the traditional lady-killer, of whom the tradition
seems to survive as a moral scarecrow for the
education of the young, though the creature is
extinct among Anglo-Saxons. He was, on the
contrary, a manly man, who looked as though he
would prefer tennis to tea and polo to poetry —
and men to women for company, as a rule. She
felt that if she had not heard him talking with
the lady in white she should have liked him
very much. As it was, she said to herself that
she wished she might never see him again — and
all the time her eyes returned again and again
to his sunburnt face and profile, till in a few
minutes she knew his features by heart.

CHAPTER IV

A CHANCE acquaintance may, under favourable circumstances, develop faster than one brought about by formal introduction, because neither party has been previously led to expect anything of the other. There is no surer way of making friendship impossible than telling two people that they are sure to be such good friends, and are just suited to each other. The law of natural selection applies to almost everything we want in the world, from food and climate to a wife.

When Clare and her mother had established themselves as usual on the terrace under the vines that afternoon, Brook came and sat beside them for a while. Mrs. Bowring liked him and talked easily with him, but Clare was silent and seemed absent-minded. The young man looked at her from time to time with curiosity, for he was not used to being treated with such perfect indifference as she showed to him. He was not spoilt, as the phrase goes, but he had always been accustomed to a certain amount of attention, when he met new people, and, without

being in the least annoyed, he thought it strange
that this particular young lady should seem not
even to listen to what he said.

Mrs. Bowring, on the other hand, scarcely
took her eyes from his face after the first ten
minutes, and not a word he spoke escaped her.
By contrast with her daughter's behaviour, her
earnest attention was very noticeable. By degrees she began to ask him questions about himself.

"Do you expect your people to-morrow?"
she inquired.

Clare looked up quickly. It was very unlike
her mother to show even that small amount of
curiosity about a stranger. It was clear that
Mrs. Bowring had conceived a sudden liking for
the young man.

"They were to have been here to-day," he
answered indifferently. "They may come this
evening, I suppose, but they have not even
ordered rooms. I asked the man there — the
owner of the place, I suppose he is."

"Then of course you will wait for them,"
suggested Mrs. Bowring.

"Yes. It's an awful bore, too. That is — "
he corrected himself hastily — "I mean, if I were
to be here without a soul to speak to, you know.
Of course, it's different, this way."

"How?" asked Mrs. Bowring, with a brighter

smile than Clare had seen on her face for a long time.

"Oh, because you are so kind as to let me talk to you," answered the young man, without the least embarrassment.

"Then you are a social person?" Mrs. Bowring laughed a little. "You don't like to be alone?"

"Oh no! Not when I can be with nice people. Of course not. I don't believe anybody does. Unless I'm doing something, you know — shooting, or going up a hill, or fishing. Then I don't mind. But of course I would much rather be alone than with bores, don't you know? Or — or — well, the other kind of people."

"What kind?" asked Mrs. Bowring.

"There are only two kinds," answered Brook, gravely. "There is our kind — and then there is the other kind. I don't know what to call them, do you? All the people who never seem to understand exactly what we are talking about nor why we do things — and all that. I call them 'the other kind.' But then I haven't a great command of language. What should you call them?"

"Cads, perhaps," suggested Clare, who had not spoken for a long time.

"Oh no, not exactly," answered the young man, looking at her. "Besides, 'cads' doesn't

include women, does it? A gentleman's son
sometimes turns out a most awful cad, a regular
'bounder.' It's rare, but it does happen sometimes. A mere cad may know, and understand
all right, but he's got the wrong sort of feeling inside of him about most things. For instance — you don't mind? A cad may know
perfectly well that he ought not to 'kiss and
tell' — but he will all the same. The 'other
kind,' as I call them, don't even know. That
makes them awfully hard to get on with."

"Then, of the two, you prefer the cad?" inquired Clare coolly.

"No. I don't know. They are both pretty
bad. But a cad may be very amusing, sometimes."

"When he kisses and tells?" asked the
young girl viciously.

Brook looked at her, in quick surprise at her
tone.

"No," he answered quietly. "I didn't mean
that. The clowns in the circus represent amusing cads. Some of them are awfully clever,
too," he added, turning the subject. "Some of
those fiddling fellows are extraordinary. They
really play very decently. They must have a
lot of talent, when you think of all the different
things they do besides their feats of strength —
they act, and play the fiddle, and sing, and
dance — "

"You seem to have a great admiration for clowns," observed Clare in an indifferent tone.

"Well — they are amusing, aren't they? Of course, it isn't high art, and that sort of thing, but one laughs at them, and sometimes they do very pretty things. One can't be always on one's hind legs, doing Hamlet, can one? There's a limit to the amount of tragedy one can stand during life. After all, it is better to laugh than to cry."

"When one can," said Mrs. Bowring thoughtfully.

"Some people always can, whatever happens," said the young girl.

"Perhaps they are right," answered the young man. "Things are not often so serious as they are supposed to be. It's like being in a house that's supposed to be haunted — on All Hallow E'en, for instance — it's awfully gruesome and creepy at night when the wind moans and the owls screech. And then, the next morning, one wonders how one could have been such an idiot. Other things are often like that. You think the world's coming to an end — and then it doesn't, you know. It goes on just the same. You are rather surprised at first, but you soon get used to it. I suppose that is what is meant by losing one's illusions."

"Sometimes the world stops for an individual

and doesn't go on again," said Mrs. Bowring, with a faint smile.

"Oh, I suppose people do break their hearts sometimes," returned Brook, somewhat thoughtfully. "But it must be something tremendously serious," he added with instant cheerfulness. "I don't believe it happens often. Most people just have a queer sensation in their throat for a minute, and they smoke a cigarette for their nerves, and go away and think of something else."

Clare looked at him, and her eyes flashed angrily, for she remembered Lady Fan's cigarette and the preceding evening. He remembered it too, and was thinking of it, for he smiled as he spoke and looked away at the horizon as though he saw something in the air. For the first time in her life the young girl had a cruel impulse. She wished that she were a great beauty, or that she possessed infinite charm, that she might revenge the little lady in white and make the man suffer as he deserved. At one moment she was ashamed of the wish, and then again it returned, and she smiled as she thought of it.

She was vaguely aware, too, that the man attracted her in a way which did not interfere with her resentment against him. She would certainly not have admitted that he was interesting to her on account of Lady Fan — but there was in her a feminine willingness to play with the fire at which another woman had burned her wings. Almost all women feel that, until they have once felt too much themselves. The more innocent and inexperienced they are, the more sure they are, as a rule, of their own perfect safety, and the more ready to run any risk.

Neither of the women answered the young man's rather frivolous assertion for some moments. Then Mrs. Bowring looked at him kindly, but with a far-away expression, as though she were thinking of some one else.

" You are young," she said gently.

" It's true that I'm not very old," he answered. " I was five-and-twenty on my last birthday."

" Five-and-twenty," repeated Mrs. Bowring very slowly, and looking at the distance, with the air of a person who is making a mental calculation.

" Are you surprised?" asked the young man, watching her.

She started a little.

"Surprised? Oh dear no! Why should I be?"

And again she looked at him earnestly, until, realising what she was doing, she suddenly shut her eyes, shook herself almost imperceptibly, and took out some work which she had brought out with her.

"Oh!" he exclaimed. "I thought you might fancy I was a good deal older or younger. But I'm always told that I look just my age."

"I think you do," answered Mrs. Bowring, without looking up.

Clare glanced at his face again. It was natural, under the circumstances, though she knew his features by heart already. She met his eyes, and for a moment she could not look away from them. It was as though they fixed her against her will, after she had once met them. There was nothing extraordinary about them, except that they were very bright and clear. With an effort she turned away, and the faint colour rose in her face.

"I am nineteen," she said quietly, as though she were answering a question.

"Indeed?" exclaimed Brook, not thinking of anything else to say.

Mrs. Bowring looked at her daughter in considerable surprise. Then Clare blushed painfully, realising that she had spoken without any intention of speaking, and had volunteered a piece of information which had certainly not been asked. It was very well, being but nineteen years old; but she was oddly conscious that if she had been forty she should have said so in just the same absent-minded way, at that moment.

"Nineteen and six are twenty-five, aren't they?" asked Mrs. Bowring suddenly.

"Yes, I believe so," answered the young man, with a laugh, but a good deal surprised in his turn, for the question seemed irrelevant and absurd in the extreme. "But I'm not good at sums," he added. "I was an awful idiot at school. They used to call me Log. That was short for logarithm, you know, because I was such a log at arithmetic. A fellow gave me the nickname one day. It wasn't very funny, so I punched his head. But the name stuck to me. Awfully appropriate, anyhow, as it turned out."

"Did you punch his head because it wasn't funny?" asked Clare, glad of the turn in the conversation.

"Oh — I don't know — on general principles. He was a diabolically clever little chap, though he wasn't very witty. He came out Senior Wrangler at Cambridge. I heard he had gone mad last year. Lots of those clever chaps do, you know. Or else they turn parsons and take pupils for a living. I'd much rather be stupid, myself. There's more to live for, when you don't know everything. Don't you think so?"

Both women laughed, and felt that the man was tactful. They were also both reflecting, of themselves and of each other, that they were not generally silly women, and they wondered

how they had both managed to say such foolish
things, speaking out irrelevantly what was passing in their minds.

"I think I shall go for a walk," said Brook,
rising rather abruptly. "I'll go up the hill for
a change. Thanks awfully. Good-bye!"

He lifted his hat and went off towards the
hotel. Mrs. Bowring looked after him, but
Clare leaned back in her seat and opened a book
she had with her. The colour rose and fell in
her cheeks, and she kept her eyes resolutely bent
down.

"What a nice fellow!" exclaimed Mrs. Bowring when the young man was out of hearing.
"I wonder who he is."

"What difference can it make, what his name
is?" asked Clare, still looking down.

"What is the matter with you, child?" Mrs.
Bowring asked. "You talk so strangely to-day!"

"So do you, mother. Fancy asking him
whether nineteen and six are twenty-five!"

"For that matter, my dear, I thought it very
strange that you should tell him your age, like
that."

"I suppose I was absent-minded. Yes! I
know it was silly, I don't know why I said it.
Do you want to know his name? I'll go and
see. It must be on the board by this time, as
he is stopping here."

She rose and was going, when her mother called her back.

"Clare! Wait till he is gone, at all events! Fancy, if he saw you!"

"Oh! He won't see me! If he comes that way I'll go into the office and buy stamps."

Clare went in and looked over the square board with its many little slips for the names of the guests. Some were on visiting cards and some were written in the large, scrawling, illiterate hand of the head waiter. Some belonged to people who were already gone. It looked well, in the little hotel, to have a great many names on the list. Some seconds passed before Clare found that of the new-comer.

"Mr. Brook Johnstone."

Brook was his first name, then. It was uncommon. She looked at it fixedly. There was no address on the small, neatly engraved card. While she was looking at it a door opened quietly behind her, in the opposite side of the corridor. She paid no attention to it for a moment; then, hearing no footsteps, she instinctively turned. Brook Johnstone was standing on the threshold watching her. She blushed violently, in her annoyance, for he could not doubt but that she was looking for his name. He saw and understood, and came forward naturally, with a smile. He had a stick in his hand.

"That's me," he said, with a little laugh, tapping his card on the board with the head of his stick. "If I'd had an ounce of manners I should have managed to tell you who I was by this time. Won't you excuse me, and take this for an introduction? Johnstone — with an E at the end — Scotch, you know."

"Thanks," answered Clare, recovering from her embarrassment. "I'll tell my mother." She hesitated a moment. "And that's us," she added, laughing rather nervously and pointing out one of the cards. "How grammatical we are, aren't we?" she laughed, while he stooped and read the name which chanced to be at the bottom of the board.

"Well — what should one say? 'That's we.' It sounds just as badly. · And you can't say 'we are that,' can you? Besides, there's no one to hear us, so it makes no difference. I don't suppose that you — you and Mrs. Bowring — would care to go for a walk, would you?"

"No," answered Clare, with sudden coldness. "I don't think so, thank you. We are not great walkers."

They went as far as the door together. Johnstone bowed and walked off, and Clare went back to her mother.

"He caught me," she said, in a tone of annoyance. "You were quite right. Then he showed

me his name himself, on the board. It's Johnstone — Mr. Brook Johnstone, with an E — he
says that he is Scotch. Why — mother! Johnstone! How odd! That was the name of — "

She stopped short and looked at her mother,
who had grown unnaturally pale during the last
few seconds.

"Yes, dear. That was the name of my first
husband."

Mrs. Bowring spoke in a low voice, looking
down at her work. But her hands trembled
violently, and she was clearly making a great
effort to control herself. Clare watched her
anxiously, not at all understanding.

"Mother dear, what is it?" she asked. "The
name is only a coincidence — it's not such an
uncommon name, after all — and besides — "

"Oh, of course," said Mrs. Bowring, in a dull
tone. "It's a mere coincidence — probably no
relation. I'm nervous, to-day."

Her manner seemed unaccountable to her
daughter, except on the supposition that she
was ill. She very rarely spoke of her first husband, by whom she had no children. When she
did, she mentioned his name gravely, as one
speaks of dead persons who have been dear, but
that was all. She had never shown anything
like emotion in connection with the subject, and
the young girl avoided it instinctively, as most

G

children, of whose parents the one has been twice married, avoid the mention of the first husband or wife, who was not their father or mother.

"I wish I understood you!" exclaimed Clare.

"There's nothing to understand, dear," said Mrs. Bowring, still very pale. "I'm nervous — that's all."

Before long she left Clare by herself and went indoors, and locked herself into her room. The rooms in the old hotel were once the cells of the monks, small vaulted chambers in which there is barely space for the most necessary furniture. During nearly an hour Mrs. Bowring paced up and down, a beat of fourteen feet between the low window and the locked door. At last she stopped before the little glass, and looked at herself, and smoothed her streaked hair.

"Nineteen and six — are twenty-five," she said slowly in a low voice, and her eyes stared into their own reflection rather wildly.

Meanwhile he spent a great deal of his time with the Bowrings. -- *Page* 83.

CHAPTER V

BROOK JOHNSTONE'S people did not come on the next day, nor on the day after that, but he expressed no surprise at the delay, and did not again say that it was a bore to have to wait for them. Meanwhile he spent a great deal of his time with the Bowrings, and the acquaintance ripened quickly towards intimacy, without passing near friendship, as such acquaintance sometimes will, when it springs up suddenly in the shallow ground of an out-of-the-way hotel on the Continent.

"For Heaven's sake don't let that man fall in love with you, Clare!" said Mrs. Bowring one morning, with what seemed unnecessary vehemence.

Clare's lip curled scornfully as she thought of poor Lady Fan.

"There isn't the slightest danger of that!" she answered. "Any more than there is of my falling in love with him," she added.

"Are you sure of that?" asked her mother. "You seem to like him. Besides, he is very nice, and very good-looking."

" Oh yes — of course he is. But one doesn't necessarily fall in love with every nice and good-looking man one meets."

Thereupon Clare cut the conversation short by going off to her own room. She had been expecting for some time that her mother would make some remark about the growing intimacy with young Johnstone. To tell the truth, Mrs. Bowring had not the slightest ground for anxiety in any previous attachment of her daughter. She was beginning to wonder whether Clare would ever show any preference for any man.

But she did not at all wish to marry her at present, for she felt that life without the girl would be unbearably lonely. On the other hand, Clare had a right to marry. They were poor. A part of their little income was the pension that Mrs. Bowring had been fortunate enough to get as the widow of an officer killed in action, but that would cease at her death, as poor Captain Bowring's allowance from his family had ceased at his death. The family had objected to the marriage from the first, and refused to do anything for his child after he was gone. It would go hard with Clare if she were left alone in the world with what her mother could leave her. On the other hand, that little, or the prospect of it, was quite safe, and would make a great difference to her, as a married woman. The two lived on it, with economy. Clare could certainly dress very well on it if she married a rich man, but she could as certainly not afford to marry a poor one.

As for this young Johnstone, he had not volunteered much information about himself, and, though Mrs. Bowring sometimes asked him questions, she was extremely careful not to ask any which could be taken in the nature of an inquiry as to his prospects in life, merely because that might possibly suggest to him that she was thinking of her daughter. And when an Englishman is reticent in such matters, it is utterly impossible to guess whether he be a millionaire or a penniless younger son. Johnstone never spoke of money, in any connection. He never said that he could afford one thing or could not afford another. He talked a good deal of shooting and sport, but never hinted that his father had any land. He never mentioned a family place in the country, nor anything of the sort. He did not even tell the Bowrings to whom the yacht belonged in which he had come, though he frequently alluded to things which had been said and done by the party during a two months' cruise, chiefly in eastern waters.

The Bowrings were quite as reticent about themselves, and each respected the other's silence. Nevertheless they grew intimate, scarcely knowing how the intimacy developed. That is to say, they very quickly became accustomed, all three, to one another's society. If Johnstone was out of the hotel first, of an afternoon, he moped about with his pipe in an objectless way, as though he had lost something, until the Bowrings came out. If he was writing letters and they appeared first, they talked in detached phrases and looked often towards the door, until he came and sat down beside them.

On the third evening, at dinner, he seemed very much amused at something, and then, as though he could not keep the joke to himself, he told his companions that he had received a telegram from his father, in answer to one of his own, informing him that he had made a mistake of a whole fortnight in the date, and must amuse himself as he pleased in the interval.

"Just like me!" he observed. "I got the letter in Smyrna or somewhere — I forget — and I managed to lose it before I had read it through. But I thought I had the date all right. I'm glad, at all events. I was tired of those good people, and it's ever so much pleasanter here."

Clare's gentle mouth hardened suddenly as she thought of Lady Fan. Johnstone had been thoroughly tired of her. That was what he meant when he spoke of "those good people."

" You get tired of people easily, don't you ? " she inquired coldly.

" Oh no — not always," answered Johnstone.

By this time he was growing used to her sudden changes of manner and to the occasional scornful speeches she made. He could not understand them in the least, as may be imagined, and having considerable experience he set them down to the score of a certain girlish shyness, which showed itself in no other way. He had known women whose shyness manifested itself in saying disagreeable things for which they were sometimes sorry afterwards.

" No," he added reflectively. " I don't think I'm a very fickle person."

Clare turned upon him the terrible innocence of her clear blue eyes. She thought she knew the truth about him too, and that he could not look her in the face. But she was mistaken. He met her glance fearlessly and quietly, with a frank smile and a little wonder at its fixed scrutiny. She would not look away, rude though she might seem, nor be stared out of countenance by a man whom she believed to be false and untrue. But his eyes were very bright, and in a few seconds they began to dazzle her, and she felt her eyelids trembling violently. It was a new sensation, and a very unpleasant one.

It seemed to her that the man had suddenly got some power over her. She made a strong effort and turned away her face, and again she blushed with annoyance.

" I beg your pardon," Johnstone said quickly, in a very low voice. " I didn't mean to be so rude."

Clare said nothing as she sat beside him, but she looked at the opposite wall, and her hand made an impatient little gesture as the fingers lay on the edge of the table. Possibly, if her mother had not been on her other side, she might have answered him. As it was, she felt that she could not speak just then. She was very much disturbed, as though something new and totally unknown had got hold of her. It was not only that she hated the man for his heartlessness, while she felt that he had some sort of influence over her, which was more than mere attraction. There was something beyond, deep down in her heart, which was nameless, and painful, but which she somehow felt that she wanted. And aside from it all, she was angry with him for having stared her out of countenance, forgetting that when she had turned upon him she had meant to do the same by him, feeling quite sure that he could not look her in the face.

They spoke little during the remainder of the

meal, for Clare was quite willing to show that she was angry, though she had little right to be. After all, she had looked at him, and he had looked at her. After dinner she disappeared, and was not seen during the remainder of the evening.

When she was alone, however, she went over the whole matter thoughtfully, and she made up her mind that she had been hasty. For she was naturally just. She said to herself that she had no claim to the man's secrets, which she had learned in a way of which she was not at all proud; and that if he could keep his own counsel, he, on his side, had a right to do so. The fact that she knew him to be heartless and faithless by no means implied that he was also indiscreet, though when an individual has done anything which we think bad we easily suppose that he may do every other bad thing imaginable. Johnstone's discretion, at least, was admirable, now that she thought of it. His bright eyes and frank look would have disarmed any suspicion short of the certainty she possessed. There had not been the least contraction of the lids, the smallest change in the expression of his mouth, not the faintest increase of colour in his young face.

So much the worse, thought the young girl suddenly. He was not only bad. He was also

an accomplished actor. No doubt his eyes had
been as steady and bright and his whole face as
truthful when he had made love to Lady Fan at
sunset on the Acropolis. Somehow, the allusion
to that scene had produced a vivid impression on
Clare's mind, and she often found herself wondering what he had said, and how he had looked
just then.

Her resentment against him increased as she
thought it all over, and again she felt a longing
to be cruel to him, and to make him suffer just
what he had made Lady Fan endure.

Then she was suddenly and unexpectedly over-
come by a shamed sense of her inability to accom-
plish any such act of justice. It was as though
she had already tried, and had failed, and he
had laughed in her face and turned away. It
seemed to her that there could be nothing in
her which could appeal to such a man. There
was Lady Fan, much older, with plenty of experience, doubtless; and she had been deceived, and
betrayed, and abandoned, before the young girl's
very eyes. What chance could such a mere girl
possibly have? It was folly, and moreover it
was wicked of her to think of such things. She
would be willingly lowering herself to his level,
trying to do the very thing which she despised
and hated in him, trying to outwit him, to out-
deceive him, to out-betray him. One side of

her nature, at least, revolted against any such scheme. Besides, she could never do it.

She was not a great beauty; she was not extraordinarily clever — not clever at all, she said to herself in her sudden fit of humility; she had no "experience." That last word means a good deal more to most young girls than they can find in it after life's illogical surprises have taught them the terrible power of chance and mood and impulse.

She glanced at her face in the mirror, and looked away. Then she glanced again. The third time she turned to the glass she began to examine her features in detail. Lady Fan was a fair woman, too. But, without vanity, she had to admit that she was much better-looking than Lady Fan. She was also much younger and fresher, which should be an advantage, she thought. She wished that her hair were golden instead of flaxen; that her eyes were dark instead of blue; that her cheeks were not so thin, and her throat a shade less slender. Nevertheless, she would have been willing to stand any comparison with the little lady in white. Of course, compared with the famous beauties, some of whom she had seen, she was scarcely worth a glance. Doubtless, Brook Johnstone knew them all.

Then she gazed into her own eyes. She did

not know that a woman, alone, may look into
her own eyes and blush and turn away. She
looked long and steadily, and quite quietly.
After all, they looked dark, for the pupils were
very large and the blue iris was of that deep
colour which borders upon violet. There was
something a little unusual in them, too, though
she could not quite make out what it was.
Why did not all women look straight before
them as she did? There must be some mysteri-
ous reason. It was a pity that her eyelashes
were almost white. Yet they, too, added something to the peculiarity of that strange gaze.

"They are like periwinkles in a snowstorm!"
exclaimed Clare, tired of her own face; and she
turned from the mirror and went to bed.

CHAPTER VI

THE first sign that two people no longer stand to each other in the relation of mere acquaintances is generally that the tones of their voices change, while they feel a slight and unaccountable constraint when they happen to be left alone together.

Two days passed after the little incident which had occurred at dinner before Clare and Johnstone were momentarily face to face out of Mrs. Bowring's sight. At first Clare had not been aware that her mother was taking pains to be always present when the young man was about, but when she noticed the fact she at once began to resent it. Such constant watchfulness was unlike her mother, un-English, and almost unnatural. When they were all seated together on the terrace, if Mrs. Bowring wished to go indoors to write a letter or to get something she invented some excuse for making her daughter go with her, and stay with her till she came out again. A French or Italian mother could not have been more particular or careful, but a French or Italian girl would have been accus-

tomed to such treatment, and would not have
seen anything unusual in it. But Mrs. Bowring
had never acted in such a way before now, and
it irritated the young girl extremely. She felt
that she was being treated like a child, and that
Johnstone must see it and think it ridiculous.
At last Clare made an attempt at resistance, out
of sheer contrariety.

" I don't want to write letters ! " she answered
impatiently. " I wrote two yesterday. It is hot
indoors, and I would much rather stay here ! "

Mrs. Bowring went as far as the parapet, and
looked down at the sea for a moment. Then
she came back and sat down again.

" It's quite true," she said. " It is hot indoors. I don't think I shall write, after all."

Brook Johnstone could not help smiling a
little, though he turned away his face to hide
his amusement. It was so perfectly evident
that Mrs. Bowring was determined not to leave
Clare alone with him that he must have been
blind not to see it. Clare saw the smile, and
was angry. She was nineteen years old, she
had been out in the world, the terrace was a
public place, Johnstone was a gentleman, and
the whole thing was absurd. She took up her
work and closed her lips tightly.

Johnstone felt the awkwardness, rose suddenly,
and said he would go for a walk. Clare raised

her eyes and nodded as he lifted his hat.   He
was still smiling, and her resentment deepened.
A moment later, mother and daughter were
alone.   Clare did not lay down her work, nor
look up when she spoke.

"Really, mother, it's too absurd!" she exclaimed, and a little colour came to her cheeks.

"What is absurd, my dear?" asked Mrs.
Bowring, affecting not to understand.

"Your abject fear of leaving me for five
minutes with Mr. Johnstone.   I'm not a baby.
He was laughing.   I was positively ashamed!
What do you suppose could have happened, if
you had gone in and written your letters and
left us quietly here?   And it happens every
day, you know!   If you want a glass of water,
I have to go in with you."

"My dear!   What an exaggeration!"

"It's not an exaggeration, mother — really.
You know that you wouldn't leave me with him
for five minutes, for anything in the world."

"Do you wish to be left alone with him, my
dear?" asked Mrs. Bowring, rather abruptly.

Clare was indignant.

"Wish it?   No!   Certainly not!   But if it should
happen naturally, by accident, I should not get
up and run away.   I'm not afraid of the man,
as you seem to be.   What can he do to me?
And you have no idea how strangely you behave,

and what ridiculous excuses you invent for me. The other day you insisted on my going in to look for a train in the' time-tables when you know we haven't the slightest intention of going away for ever so long. Really — you're turning into a perfect duenna. I wish you would behave naturally, as you always used to do."

"I think you exaggerate," said Mrs. Bowring. "I never leave you alone with men you hardly know — "

"You can't exactly say that we hardly know Mr. Johnstone, when he has been with us, morning, noon, and night, for nearly a week, mother."

"My dear, we know nothing about him — "

"If you are so anxious to know his father's Christian name, ask him. It wouldn't seem at all odd. I will, if you like."

"Don't!" cried Mrs. Bowring, with unusual energy. "I mean," she added in a lower tone and looking away, "it would be very rude — he would think it very strange. In fact, it is merely idle curiosity on my part — really, I would much rather not know."

Clare looked at her mother in surprise.

"How oddly you talk!" she exclaimed. Then her tone changed. "Mother dear — is anything the matter? You don't seem quite — what shall I say? Are you suffering, dearest? Has anything happened?"

She dropped her work and leaned forward, her hand on her
mother's. — *Page* 97.

She dropped her work, and leaned forward, her hand on her mother's, and gazing into her face with a look of anxiety.

"No, dear," answered Mrs. Bowring. "No, no — it's nothing. Perhaps I'm a little nervous — that's all."

"I believe the air of this place doesn't suit you. Why shouldn't we go away at once?"

Mrs. Bowring shook her head and protested energetically.

"No — oh no! I wouldn't go away for anything. I like the place immensely, and we are both getting perfectly well here. Oh no! I wouldn't think of going away."

Clare leaned back in her seat again. She was devotedly fond of her mother, and she could not but see that something was wrong. In spite of what she said, Mrs. Bowring was certainly not growing stronger, though she was not exactly ill. The pale face was paler, and there was a worn and restless look in the long-suffering, almost colourless eyes.

"I'm sorry I made such a fuss about Mr. Johnstone," said Clare softly, after a short pause.

"No, darling," answered her mother instantly. "I dare say I have been a little over careful. I don't know — I had a sort of presentiment that you might take a fancy to him."

"I know. You said so the first day. But I

H

sha'n't, mother. You need not be at all afraid.
He is not at all the sort of man to whom I should
ever take a fancy, as you call it."

" I don't see why not," said Mrs. Bowring
thoughtfully.

" Of course — it's hard to explain." Clare
smiled. " But if that is what you are afraid of,
you can leave us alone all day. My 'fancy'
would be quite, quite different."

" Very well, darling. At all events, I'll try
not to turn into a duenna."

Johnstone did not appear again until dinner,
and then he was unusually silent, only exchanging a remark with Clare now and then, and not
once leaning forward to say a few words to Mrs.
Bowring as he generally did. The latter had
at first thought of exchanging places with her
daughter, but had reflected that it would be
almost a rudeness to make such a change after
the second day.

They went out upon the terrace, and had
their coffee there. Several of the other people
did the same, and walked slowly up and down
under the vines. Mrs. Bowring, wishing to destroy as soon as possible the unpleasant impression she had created, left the two together,
saying that she would get something to put
over her shoulders, as the air was cool.

Clare and Johnstone stood by the parapet and

Johnstone sat down upon the wall, while Clare leaned over it. — *Page* 99.

looked at each other. Then Clare leaned with her elbows on the wall and stared in silence at the little lights on the beach below, trying to make out the shapes of the boats which were hauled up in a long row. Neither spoke for a long time, and Clare, at least, felt unpleasantly the constraint of the unusual silence.

"It is a beautiful place, isn't it?" observed Johnstone at last, for the sake of hearing his own voice.

"Oh yes, quite beautiful," answered the young girl in a half-indifferent, half-discontented tone, and the words ended with a sort of girlish sniff.

Again there was silence. Johnstone, standing up beside her, looked towards the hotel, to see whether Mrs. Bowring were coming back. But she was anxious to appear indifferent to their being together, and was in no hurry to return. Johnstone sat down upon the wall, while Clare leaned over it.

"Miss Bowring!" he said suddenly, to call her attention.

"Yes?" She did not look up; but to her own amazement she felt a queer little thrill at the sound of his voice, for it had not its usual tone.

"Don't you think I had better go to Naples?" he asked.

Clare felt herself start a little, and she waited a moment before she said anything in reply. She did not wish to betray any astonishment in her voice. Johnstone had asked the question under a sudden impulse; but a far wiser and more skilful man than himself could not have hit upon one better calculated to precipitate intimacy. Clare, on her side, was woman enough to know that she had a choice of answers, and to see that the answer she should choose must make a difference hereafter. At the same time, she had been surprised, and when she thought of it afterwards it seemed to her that the question itself had been an impertinent one, merely because it forced her to make an answer of some sort. She decided in favour of making everything as clear as possible.

"Why?" she asked, without looking round.

At all events she would throw the burden of an elucidation upon him. He was not afraid of taking it up.

"It's this," he answered. "I've rather thrust my acquaintance upon you, and, if I stay here until my people come, I can't exactly change my seat and go and sit at the other end of the table, nor pretend to be busy all day, and never come out here and sit with you, after telling you repeatedly that I have nothing on earth to do. Can I?"

"Why should you?"

"Because Mrs. Bowring doesn't like me."

Clare rose from her elbows and stood up, resting her hands upon the wall, but still looking down at the lights on the beach.

"I assure you, you're quite mistaken," she answered, with quiet emphasis. "My mother thinks you're very nice."

"Then why—" Johnstone checked himself, and crumbled little bits of mortar from the rough wall with his thumbs.

"Why what?"

"I don't know whether I know you well enough to ask the question, Miss Bowring."

"Let's assume that you do—for the sake of argument," said Clare, with a short laugh, as she glanced at his face, dimly visible in the falling darkness.

"Thanks awfully," he answered, but he did not laugh with her. "It isn't exactly an easy thing to say, is it? Only—I couldn't help noticing—I hope you'll forgive me, if you think I'm rude, won't you? I couldn't help noticing that your mother was most awfully afraid of leaving us alone for a minute, you know — as though she thought I were a suspicious character, don't you know? Something of that sort. So, of course, I thought she didn't like me. Do you see? Tremendously cheeky of me to talk in this way, isn't it?"

"Do you know? It is, rather." Clare was more inclined to laugh than before, but she only smiled in the dark.

"Well, it would be, of course, if I didn't happen to be so painfully respectable."

"Painfully respectable! What an expression!" This time, Clare laughed aloud.

"Yes. That's just it. Well, I couldn't exactly tell Mrs. Bowring that, could I? Besides, one isn't vain of being respectable. I couldn't say, Please, Mrs. Bowring, my father is Mr. Smith, and my mother was a Miss Brown, of very good family, and we've got five hundred a year in Consols, and we're not in trade, and I've been to a good school, and am not at all dangerous. It would have sounded so — so uncalled for, don't you know? Wouldn't it?"

"Very. But now that you've explained it to me, I suppose I may tell my mother, mayn't I? Let me see. Your father is Mr. Smith, and your mother was a Miss Brown—"

"Oh, please—no!" interrupted Johnstone. "I didn't mean it so very literally. But it is just about that sort of thing—just like anybody else. Only about our not being in trade, I'm not so sure of that. My father is a brewer. Brewing is not a profession, so I suppose it must be a trade, isn't it?"

"You might call it a manufacture," suggested Clare.

"Yes. It sounds better. But that isn't the question, you know. You'll see my people when they come, and then you'll understand what I mean — they really are tremendously respectable."

"Of course!" assented the young girl. "Like the party you came with on the yacht. That kind of people."

"Oh dear no!" exclaimed Johnstone. "Not at all those kind of people. They wouldn't like it at all, if you said so."

"Ah! indeed!" Clare was inclined to laugh again.

"The party I came with belong rather to a gay set. Awfully nice, you know," he hastened to add, "and quite the people one knows at home. But my father and mother — oh no! they are quite different — the difference between whist and baccarat, you know, if you understand that sort of thing — old port and brandy and soda — both very good in their way, but quite different."

"I should think so."

"Then —" Johnstone hesitated again. "Then, Miss Bowring — you don't think that your mother really dislikes me, after all?"

"Oh dear no! Not in the least. I've heard her say all sorts of nice things about you."

"Really? Then I think I'll stay here. I didn't want to be a nuisance, you know — always in the way."

"You're not in the way," answered Clare.

Mrs. Bowring came back with her shawl, and the rest of the evening passed off as usual. Later, when she was alone, the young girl remembered all the conversation, and she saw that it had been in her power to make Johnstone leave Amalfi. While she was wondering why she had not done so, since she hated him for what she knew of him, she fell asleep, and the question remained unanswered. In the morning she told the substance of it all to her mother, and ended by telling her that Johnstone's father was a brewer.

"Of course," answered Mrs. Bowring absently. "I know that." Then she realised what she had said, and glanced at Clare with an odd, scared look.

Clare uttered an exclamation of surprise.

"Mother! Why, then — you knew all about him! Why didn't you tell me?"

A long silence followed, during which Mrs. Bowring sat with her face turned from her daughter. Then she raised her hand and passed it slowly over her forehead, as though trying to collect her thoughts.

"One comes across very strange things in

life, my dear," she said at last. "I am not sure that we had not better go away, after all. I'll think about it."

Beyond this Clare could get no information, nor any explanation of the fact that Mrs. Bowring should have known something about Brook Johnstone's father. The girl made a guess, of course. The elder Johnstone must be a relation of her mother's first husband ; though, considering that Mrs. Bowring had never seen Brook before now, and that the latter had never told her anything about his father, it was hard to see how she could be so sure of the fact. Possibly, Brook strongly resembled his father's family. That, indeed, was the only admissible theory. But all that Clare knew and could put together into reasonable shape could not explain why her mother so much disliked leaving her alone with the man, even for five minutes.

In this, however, Mrs. Bowring changed suddenly, after the first evening when she had left them on the terrace. She either took a totally different view of the situation, or else she was ashamed of seeming to watch them all the time, and the consequence was that during the next three or four days they were very often together without her.

Johnstone enjoyed the young girl's society, and did not pretend to deny the fact in his own thoughts. Whatever mischief he might have been in while on the yacht, his natural instincts were simple and honest. In a certain way, Clare was a revelation to him of something to which he had never been accustomed, and which he had most carefully avoided. He had no sisters, and as a boy he had not been thrown with girls. He was an only son, and his mother, a very practical woman, had warned him as he grew up that he was a great match, and had better avoid young girls altogether until he saw one whom he should like to marry, though how he was to see that particular one, if he avoided all alike, was a question into which his mother did not choose to enter. Having first gone into society upon this principle, however, and having been at once taken up and made much of by an extremely fashionable young woman afflicted with an elderly and eccentric husband, it was not likely that Brook would return to the threshold of the schoolroom for women's society. He went on as he had begun in his first "salad" days, and at five-and-twenty he had the reputation of having done more damage than any of his young contemporaries, while he had never once shown the slightest inclination to marry. His mother, always a practical woman, did not press the question of marriage, deeming that with his disposition he would stand a better chance of married peace when he had expended a good deal of what she called his vivacity; and his father, who came of very long-lived people, always said that no man should take a wife before he was thirty. As Brook did not gamble immoderately, nor start a racing stable, nor propose to manage an opera troupe, the practical lady felt that he was really a very good young man. His father liked him for his own sake; but as Adam Johnstone had been gay in his youth, in spite of his sober Scotch blood, even beyond the bounds of ordinary "fastness," the fact of his being fond of Brook was not of itself a guarantee that the latter was such a very good young man as his mother said that he was. Somehow or other Brook had hitherto managed to keep clear of any entanglement which could. hamper his life, probably by virtue of that hardness which he had shown to poor Lady Fan, and which had so strongly prejudiced Clare Bowring against him. His father said cynically that the lad was canny. Hitherto he had certainly shown that he could be selfish; and perhaps there is less difference between the meanings of the Scotch and English words than most people suppose.

Daily and almost hourly intercourse with such a young girl as Clare was a totally new experience to Brook Johnstone, and there were

moments when he hardly recognised himself for
the man who had landed from the yacht ten
days earlier, and who had said good-bye to Lady
Fan on the platform behind the hotel.

Hitherto he had always known in a day or
two whether he was inclined to make love to a
woman or not. An inclination to make love
and the satisfaction of it had been, so far, his
nearest approach to being in love at all. Nor,
when he had felt the inclination, had he ever
hesitated. Like a certain great English states-
man of similar disposition, he had sometimes
been repulsed, but he never remembered having
given offence. For he possessed that tactful
intuition which guides some men through life in
their intercourse with women. He rarely spoke
the first word too soon, and if he were going to
speak at all he never spoke too late — which
error is, of the two, by far the greater. He
was young, perhaps, to have had such experience; but in the social world of to-day it is
especially the fashion for men to be extremely
young, even to youthfulness, and lack of years
is no longer the atrocious crime which Pitt
would neither attempt to palliate or deny.
We have just emerged from a period of wrinkles
and paint, during which we were told that age
knew everything and youth nothing. The ex-
plosion into nonsense of nine tenths of all we

were taught at school and college has given our children a terrible weapon against us; and women, who are all practical in their own way, prefer the blundering whole-heartedness of youth to the skilful tactics and over-effective effects of the middle-aged love-actor. In this direction, at least, the breeze that goes before the dawn of a new century is already blowing. Perhaps it is a good sign — but a sign of some sort it certainly is.

Brook Johnstone felt that he was in an unfamiliar position, and he tried to analyse his own feelings. He was perfectly honest about it, but he had very little talent for analysis. On the other hand, he had a very keen sense of what we roughly call honour. Clare was not Lady Fan, and would probably never get into that category. Clare belonged amongst the women whom he respected, and he respected them all, with all his heart. They included all young girls, and his mother, and all young women who were happily married. It will be admitted that, for a man who made no pretence to higher virtues, Brook was no worse than his contemporaries, and was better than a great many.

Be that as it may, in lack of any finer means of discrimination, he tried to define his own position with regard to Clare Bowring very simply and honestly. Either he was falling in love,

or he was not. Secondly, Clare was either the
kind of girl whom he should like to marry,
spoken of by his practical mother—or she was
not.

So far, all was extremely plain. The trouble
was that he could not find any answers to the
questions. He could not in the least be sure
that he was falling in love, because he knew
that he had never really been in love in his life.
And as for saying at once that Clare was, or
was not, the girl whom he should like to marry,
how in the world could he tell that, unless he
fell in love with her? Of course he did not
wish to marry her unless he loved her. But he
conceived it possible that he might fall in love
with her and then not wish to marry her after
all, which, in his simple opinion, would have
been entirely despicable. If there were any
chance of that, he ought to go away at once.
But he did not know whether there were any
chance of it or not. He could go away in any
case, in order to be on the safe side; but then,
there was no reason in the world why he should
not marry her, if he should love her, and if she
would marry him. The question became very
badly mixed, and under the circumstances he
told himself that he was splitting hairs on the
mountains he had made of his molehills. He
determined to stay where he was. At all events,

judging from all signs with which he was acquainted, Clare was very far indeed from being in love with him, so that in this respect his sense of honour was perfectly safe and undisturbed.

Having set his mind at rest in this way, he allowed himself to talk with her as he pleased. There was no reason why he should hamper himself in conversation, so long as he said nothing calculated to make an impression — nothing which could come under the general head of " making love." The result was that he was much more agreeable than he supposed. Clare's innocent eyes watched him, and her mind was divided about him.

She was utterly young and inexperienced, but she was a woman, and she believed him to be false, faithless, and designing. She had no idea of the broad distinction he drew between all good and innocent women like herself, and all the rest whom he considered lawful prey. She concluded therefore, very rashly, that he was simply pursuing his usual tactics, a main part of which consisted in seeming perfectly unaffected and natural while only waiting for a faint sign of encouragement in order then to play the part of the passionate lover.

The generalisations of youth are terrible. What has failed once is despicably damned for ever. What is true to-day is true enough to-morrow to kill all other truths outright. The man whose hand has shaken once is a coward; he who has fought one battle is to be the hero of seventy. Life is a forest of inverted pyramids, for the young; upon every point is balanced a gigantic weight of top-heavy ideals, spreading base-upwards.

To Clare, everything Johnstone said or did was the working of a faithless intention towards its end. It was clear enough that he sought her and stayed with her as long as he could, day by day. Therefore he intended to make love to her, sooner or later, and then, when he was tired, he would say good-bye to her just as he had said good-bye to Lady Fan, and break her heart, and have one story more to laugh over when he was alone. It was quite clear that he could not mean anything else, after what she had seen.

All the same, he pleased her when he was with her, and attracted her oddly. She told herself that unless he had some unusual qualities he could not possibly break hearts for pastime, as he undoubtedly did, from year's end to year's end. She studied the question, and reached the conclusion that his strength was in his eyes. They were the most frank, brave, good-humoured, clear, unaffected eyes she had ever seen, but she could not look at them long. There was no reason why she should, indeed, but she hated to feel that she could not, if she chose. Whenever she tried, she at once had the feeling that he had power over her, to make her do things she did not wish to do. That was probably the way in which he had influenced Lady Fan and the other women, probably a dozen, thought Clare. If they were really as honest as they seemed, she thought she should have been able to meet them without the least sensation of nervousness.

One day she caught herself wishing that he had never done the thing she so hated. She was too honest to attribute to him outward defects which he did not possess, and she could not help thinking what a fine fellow he would be if he were not so bad. She might have liked him very much, then. But as it was, it was impossible that she should ever not hate him. Then she smiled to herself, as she thought how surprised he would be if he could guess what she thought of him.

But there was no probability of that, for she felt that she had no right to know what she knew, and so she treated him always, as she thought, with the same even, indifferent civility. But not seldom she knew that she was wickedly wishing that he might really fall in love with her and find out that men could break their hearts as well as women. She should like to fight with him, with his own weapons, for the glory of all her sex, and make him thoroughly miserable for his sins. It could not be wrong to wish that, after what she had seen, but it would be very wrong to try and make him fall in love, just with that intention. That would be almost as bad as what he had done; not quite so bad, of course, because it would serve him right, but yet a deed which she might be ashamed to remember.

She herself felt perfectly safe. She was neither sentimental nor susceptible, for if she had been one or the other she must by this time have had some "experience," as she vaguely called it. But she had not. She had never even liked any man so much as she liked this man whom she hated. This was not a contradiction of facts, which, as Euclid teaches us, is impossible. She liked him for what she saw, and she hated him for what she knew.

One day, when Mrs. Bowring was present, the conversation turned upon a recent novel in which the hero, after making love to a woman, found that he had made a mistake, and promptly made love to her sister, whom he married in the end.

"I despise that sort of man!" cried Clare, rather vehemently, and flashing her eyes upon Johnstone.

For a moment she had thought that she could surprise him, that he would look away, or change colour, or in some way betray his most guilty conscience. But he did not seem in the least disturbed, and met her glance as calmly as ever.

"Do you?" he asked with an indifferent laugh. "Why? The fellow was honest, at all events. He found that he didn't love the one to whom he was engaged, and that he did love the other. So he set things straight before it was too late, and married the right one. He was a very sensible man, and it must have taken courage to be so honest about it."

"Courage!" exclaimed the young girl in high scorn. "He was a brute and a coward!"

"Dear me!" laughed Brook. "Don't you admit that a man may ever make a mistake?"

"When a man makes a mistake of that sort, he should either cut his throat, or else keep his word to the woman and try to make her happy."

"That's a violent view — really! It seems to me that when a man has made a mistake the best thing to do is to go and say so. The bigger the mistake, the harder it is to acknowledge it, and the more courage it needs. Don't you think so, Mrs. Bowring?"

"The mistake of all mistakes is a mistake in marriage," said the elder woman, looking away. "There is no remedy for that, but death."

"Yes," answered Clare. "But don't you think that I'm right? It's what you say, after all —"

"Not exactly, my dear. No man who doesn't love a woman can make her happy for long."

"Well — a man who makes a woman think that he loves her, and then leaves her for some one else, is a brute, and a beast, and a coward, and a wretch, and a villain — and I hate him, and so do all women!"

"That's categorical!" observed Brook, with a laugh. "But I dare say you are quite right in theory, only practice is so awfully different, you know. And a woman doesn't thank a man for pretending to love her."

Clare's eyes flashed almost savagely, and her lip curled in scorn.

"There's only one right," she said. "I don't know how many wrongs there are — and I don't want to know!"

"No," answered Brook, gravely enough. "And there is no reason why you ever should."

CHAPTER VII

"You seemed to be most tremendously in earnest yesterday, when we were talking about that book," observed Brook on the following afternoon.

"Of course I was," answered Clare. "I said just what I thought."

They were walking together along the high road which leads from Amalfi towards Salerno. It is certainly one of the most beautiful roads in Europe, and in the whole world. The chain of rocky heights dashes with wild abruptness from its five thousand feet straight to the dark-blue sea, bristling with sharp needles and spikes of stone, rough with a chaos of brown boulders, cracked from peak to foot with deep torn gorges. In each gorge nestles a garden of orange and lemons and pomegranates, and out of the stones there blows a perfume of southern blossom through all the month of May. The sea lies dark and clear below, ever tideless, often still as a woodland pool; then, sometimes, it rises suddenly in deep-toned wrath, smiting the face of the cliff, booming through the low-mouthed caves, curling its great green curls and combing them out to frothing ringlets along the strips of beach, winding itself about the rock of Conca in a heavily gleaming sheet and whirling its wraith of foam to heaven, the very ghost of storm.

And in the face of those rough rocks, high above the water, is hewn a way that leads round the mountain's base, many miles along it, over the sharp-jutting spurs, and in between the boulders and the needles, down into the gardens of the gorges and past the dark towers whence watchmen once descried the Saracen's ill-boding sail and sent up their warning beacon of smoke by day and fire by night.

It is the most beautiful road in the world, in its infinite variety, in the grandeur above and the breadth below, and the marvellous rich sweetness of the deep gardens — passing as it does out of wilderness into splendour, out of splendour into wealth of colour and light and odour, and again out to the rugged strength of the loneliness beyond.

Clare and Johnstone had exchanged idle phrases for a while, until they had passed Atrani and the turn where the new way leads up to Ravello, and were fairly out on the road. They were both glad to be out together and walking, for Clare had grown stronger, and was weary of always sitting on the terrace, and

Johnstone was tired of taking long walks alone, merely for the sake of being hungry afterwards, and of late had given it up altogether. Mrs. Bowring herself was glad to be alone for once, and made little or no objection, and so the two had started in the early afternoon.

Johnstone's remark had been premeditated, for his curiosity had been aroused on the preceding day by Clare's words and manner. But after she had given him her brief answer she said no more, and they walked on in silence for a few moments.

"Yes," said Johnstone at last, as though he had been reflecting, "you generally say what you think. I didn't doubt it at the time. But you seem rather hard on the men. Women are all angels, of course —"

"Not at all!" interrupted Clare. "Some of us are quite the contrary."

"Well, it's a generally accepted thing, you know. That's what I mean. But it isn't generally accepted that men are. If you take men into consideration at all, you must make some allowances."

"I don't see why. You are much stronger than we are. You all think that you have much more pride. You always say that you have a sense of honour which we can't understand. I should think that with all those advantages you would be much too proud to insist upon our making allowances for you."

"That's rather keen, you know," answered Brook, with a laugh. "All the same, it's a woman's occupation to be good, and a man has a lot of other things to do besides. That's the plain English of it. When a woman isn't good she falls. When a man is bad, he doesn't — it's his nature."

"Oh — if you begin by saying that all men are bad! That's an odd way out of it."

"Not at all. Good men and bad women are the exceptions, that's all — in the way you mean goodness and badness."

"And how do you think I mean goodness and badness? It seems to me that you are taking a great deal for granted, aren't you?"

"Oh, I don't know," said Brook, growing vague on a sudden. "Those are rather hard things to talk about."

"I like to talk about them. How do you think I understand those two words?"

"I don't know," repeated Johnstone, still more vaguely. "I suppose your theory is that men and women are exactly equal, and that a man shouldn't do what a woman ought not to do — and all that, you know. I don't exactly know how to put it."

"I don't see why what is wrong for a woman

should be right for a man," said Clare. "The
law doesn't make any difference, does it? A
man goes to prison for stealing or forging, and
so does a woman. I don't see why society
should make any distinction about other things.
If there were a law against flirting, it would
send the men to prison just like the women,
wouldn't it?"

" What an awful idea!" laughed Brook.

" Yes, but in theory—"

"Oh, in theory it's all right. But in practice
we men are not wrapped in cotton and tied up
with pink ribbons from the day we are born
to the day we are married. I — I don't exactly
know how to explain what I mean, but that's
the general idea. Among poor people — I
believe one mustn't say the lower classes any
more — well, with them it isn't quite the same.
The women don't get so much care and looking
after, when they are young, you know — that
sort of thing. The consequence is, that there's
much more equality between men and women.
I believe the women are worse, and the men are
better — it's my opinion, at all events. I dare
say it isn't worth much. It's only what I see
at home, you know."

" But the working people don't flirt!" exclaimed Clare. " They drink, and that sort of
thing — "

"Yes, lots of them drink, men and women. And as for flirting — they don't call it flirting, but in their way I dare say it's very much the same thing. Only, in our part of the country, a man who flirts, if you call it so, gets just as bad a name as a woman. You see, they have all had about the same bringing up. But with us it's quite different. A girl is brought up in a cage, like a turtle dove, with nothing to do except to be good, while a boy is sent to a public school when he is eleven or twelve, which is exactly the same as sending him to hell, except that he has the certainty of getting away."

"But boys don't learn to flirt at Eton," observed the young girl.

"Well — no," answered Johnstone. "But they learn everything else, except Latin and Greek, and they go to a private tutor to learn those things before they go to the university."

"You mean that they learn to drink and gamble, and all that?" asked Clare.

"Oh — more or less — a little of everything that does no good — and then you expect us afterwards to be the same as you are, who have been brought up by your mothers at home. It isn't fair, you know."

"No," answered Clare, yielding. "It isn't fair. That strikes me as the best argument you

have used yet.   But it doesn't make it right, for
all that.   And why shouldn't men be brought
up to be good, just as women are?"

Brook laughed.

"That's quite another matter.   Only a pater-
nal government could do that — or a maternal
government.   We haven't got either, so we have
to do the best we can.   I only state the fact,
and you are obliged to admit it.   I can't go back
to the reason.   The fact remains.   In certain
ways, at a certain age, all men as a rule are
bad, and all women, on the whole, are good.
Most of you know it, and you judge us accordingly and make allowances.   But you
yourself don't seem inclined to be merciful.
Perhaps you'll be less hard-hearted when you
are older."

"I'm not hard-hearted!" exclaimed Clare,
indignantly.   "I'm only just.   And I shall
always be the same, I'm sure."

"If I were a Frenchman," said Brook, "I
should be polite, and say that I hoped so.   As
I'm not, and as it would be rude to say that I
didn't believe it, I'll say nothing.   Only to be
what you call just, isn't the way to be liked, you
know."

"I don't want to be liked," Clare answered,
rather sharply.   "I hate what are called popular
people!"

"So do I. They are generally awful bores, don't you know? They want to keep the thing up and be liked all the time."

" Well — if one likes people at all, one ought to like them all the time," objected Clare, with unnecessary contrariety.

"That was the original point," observed Brook. " That was your objection to the man in the book — that he loved first one sister and then the other. Poor chap! The first one loved him, and the second one prayed for him! He had no luck!"

" A man who will do that sort of thing is past praying for!" retorted the young girl. " It seems to me that when a man makes a woman believe that he loves her, the best thing he can do is to be faithful to her afterwards."

" Yes — but supposing that he is quite sure that he can't make her happy —"

"Then he had no right to make love to her at all."

" But he didn't know it at first. He didn't find out until he had known her a long time."

"That makes it all the worse," exclaimed Clare with conviction, but without logic.

"And while he was trying to find out, she fell in love with him," continued Brook. " That was unlucky, but it wasn't his fault, you know —"

"Oh yes, it was — in that book at least. He asked her to marry him before he had half made up his mind. Really, Mr. Johnstone," she continued, almost losing her temper, "you defend the man almost as though you were defending yourself!"

"That's rather a hard thing to say to a man, isn't it?"

Johnstone was young enough to be annoyed, though he was amused.

"Then why do you defend the man?" asked Clare, standing still at a turn of the road and facing him.

"I won't, if we are going to quarrel about a ridiculous book," he answered, looking at her. "My opinion's not worth enough for that."

"If you have an opinion at all, it's worth fighting for."

"I don't want to fight, and I won't fight with you," he answered, beginning to laugh.

"With me or with any one else — "

"No — not with you," he said with sudden emphasis.

"Why not with me?"

"Because I like you very much," he answered boldly, and they stood looking at each other in the middle of the road.

Clare had started in surprise, and the colour rose slowly to her face, but she would not take her eyes from his. For the first time it seemed to her that he had no power over her.

"I'm sorry," she answered. "For I don't like you."

"Are you in earnest?" He could not help laughing.

"Yes." There was no mistaking her tone.

Johnstone's face changed, and for the first time in their acquaintance he was the one to turn his eyes away.

"I'm sorry too," he said quietly. "Shall we turn back?" he asked after a moment's pause.

"No, I want to walk," answered Clare.

She turned from him, and began to walk on in silence. For some time neither spoke. Johnstone was puzzled, surprised, and a little hurt, but he attributed what she had said to his own roughness in telling her that he liked her, though he could not see that he had done anything so very terrible. He had spoken spontaneously, too, without the least thought of producing an impression, or of beginning to make love to her. Perhaps he owed her an apology. If she thought so, he did, and it could do no harm to try.

"I'm very sorry, if I have offended you just now," he said gently. "I didn't mean to."

"You didn't offend me," answered Clare. "It isn't rude to say that one likes a person."

" I'm sorry, too," he said quietly.   " Shall we turn back? "— *Page* 126.

"Oh — I beg your pardon — I thought perhaps — "

He hesitated, surprised by her very unexpected answer. He could not imagine what she wanted.

"Because I said that I didn't like you?" she asked.

"Well — yes."

"Then it was I who offended you," answered the young girl. "I didn't mean to, either. Only, when you said that you liked me, I thought you were in earnest, you know, and so I wanted to be quite honest, because I thought it was fairer. You see, if I had let you think that I liked you, you might have thought we were going to drift into being friends, and that's impossible, you know — because I never did like you, and I never shall. But that needn't prevent our walking together, and talking, and all that. At least, I don't mean that it should. That's the reason why I won't turn back just yet — "

"But how in the world can you enjoy walking and talking with a man you don't like?" asked Johnstone, who was completely at sea, and began to think that he must be dreaming.

"Well — you are awfully good company, you know, and I can't always be sitting with my mother on the terrace, though we love each other dearly."

"You are the most extraordinary person!"
exclaimed Johnstone, in genuine bewilderment.
"And of course your mother dislikes me too,
doesn't she?"

"Not at all," answered Clare. "You asked
me that before, and I told you the truth. Since
then, she likes you better and better. She is
always saying how nice you are."

"Then I had better always talk to her," suggested Brook, feeling for a clue.

"Oh, I shouldn't like that at all!" cried the
young girl, laughing.

"And yet you don't like me. This is like
twenty questions. You must have some very
particular reason for it," he added thoughtfully.
"I suppose I must have done some awful thing
without knowing it. I wish you would tell me.
Won't you, please? Then I'll go away."

"No," Clare answered. "I won't tell you.
But I have a reason. I'm not capricious. I
don't take violent dislikes to people for nothing.
Let it alone. We can talk .very pleasantly
about other things. Since you are good enough
to like me, it might be amusing to tell me why.
If you have any good reason, you know, you
won't stop liking me just because I don't like
you, will you?"

She glanced sideways at him as she spoke,
and he was watching her and trying to under-

stand her, for the revelation of her dislike had come upon him very suddenly. She was on the right as they walked, and he saw her against the light sky, above the line of the low parapet. Perhaps the light behind her dazzled him; at all events, he had a strange impression for a moment. She seemed to have the better of him, and to be stronger and more determined than he. She seemed taller than she was, too, for she was on the higher part of the road, in the middle of it. For an instant he felt precisely what she so often felt with him, that she had power over him. But he did not resent the sensation as she did, though it was quite as new to him.

Nevertheless, he did not answer her, for she had spoken only half in earnest, and he himself was not just then inclined to joke for the mere sake of joking. He looked down at the road under his feet, and he knew all at once that Clare attracted him much more than he had imagined. The sidelong glance she had bestowed upon him had fascination in it. There was an odd charm about her girlish contrariety and in her frank avowal that she did not like him. Her dislike roused him. He did not choose to be disliked by her, especially for some absurd trifle in his behaviour, which he had not even noticed when he had made the mistake, whatever it might be.

K

He walked along in silence, and he was aware
of her light tread and the soft sound of her
serge skirt as she moved. He wished her to
like him, and wished that he knew what to do
to change her mind. But that would not be easy,
since he did not know the cause of her dislike.
Presently she spoke again, and more gravely.

"I should not have said that. I'm sorry.
But of course you knew that I wasn't in earnest."

"I don't know why you should not have said
it," he answered. "As a matter of fact, you are
quite right. I don't like you any the less because you don't like me. Liking isn't a bargain with cash on delivery. I think I like
you all the more for being so honest. Do you
mind?"

"Not in the least. It's a very good reason."
Clare smiled, and then suddenly looked grave
again, wondering whether it would not be really
honest to tell him then and there that she had
overheard his last interview with Lady Fan.

But she reflected that it could only make him
feel uncomfortable.

"And another reason why I like you is because you are combative," he said thoughtfully.
"I'm not, you know. One always admires the
qualities one hasn't oneself."

"And you are not combative? You don't
like to be in the opposition?"

"Not a bit! I'm not fond of fighting. I systematically avoid a row."

"I shouldn't have thought that," said Clare, looking at him again. "Do you know? I think most people would take you for a soldier."

"Do I look as though I would seek the bubble reputation at the cannon's mouth?" Brook laughed. "Am I full of strange oaths?"

"Oh, that's ridiculous, you know!" exclaimed Clare. "I mean, you look as though you would fight."

"I never would if I could help it. And so far I have managed 'to help it' very well. I'm naturally mild, I think. You are not, you know. I don't mean to be rude, but I think you are pugnacious — 'combative' is prettier."

"My father was a soldier," said the girl, with some pride.

"And mine is a brewer. There's a lot of inheritable difference between handling gunpowder and brewing mild ale. Like father, like son. I shall brew mild ale too. If you could have charged at Balaclava, you would. By the way, it isn't the beer that you object to? Please tell me. I shouldn't mind at all, and I'd much rather know that it was only that."

"How absurd!" cried Clare with scorn. "As though it made any difference!"

"Well — what is it, then?" asked Brook with

sudden impatience. "You have no right to hate me without telling me why."

"No right?" The young girl turned on him half fiercely, and then laughed. "You haven't a standing order from Heaven to be liked by the whole human race, you know!"

"And if I had, you would be the solitary exception, I suppose," suggested Johnstone with a rather discontented smile.

"Perhaps."

"Is there anything I could do to make you change your mind? Because, if it were anything in reason, I'd do it."

"It's rather a pity that you should put in the condition of its being in reason," answered Clare, as her lip curled. "But there isn't anything. You may just as well give it up at once."

"I won't."

"It's a waste of time, I assure you. Besides, it's mere vanity. It's only because everybody likes you — so you think that I should too."

"Between us, we are getting at my character at last," observed Brook with some asperity. "You've discovered my vanity, now. By-and-by we shall find out some more good qualities."

"Perhaps. Each one will be a step in our acquaintance, you know. Steps may lead down, as well as up. We are walking down hill on this road just now, and it's steep. Look at that unfortunate mule dragging that cart up hill towards us! That's like trying to be friends, against odds. I wish the man would not beat the beast like that, though! What brutes these people are!"

Her dark blue eyes fixed themselves keenly on the sight, and the pupils grew wide and angry. The cart was a hundred yards away, coming up the road, piled high with sacks of potatoes, and drawn by one wretched mule. The huge carter was sprawling on the front sacks, yelling a tuneless chant at the top of his voice. He was a black-haired man, with a hideous mouth, and his face was red with wine. As he yelled his song he flogged his miserable beast with a heavy whip, accenting his howls with cruel blows. Clare grew pale with anger as she came nearer and saw it all more distinctly. The mule's knees bent nearly double at every violent step, its wide eyes were bright red all round, its white tongue hung out, and it gasped for breath. The road was stony, too, besides being steep, for it had been lately mended and not rolled.

"Brute!" exclaimed Clare, in a low voice, and her face grew paler.

Johnstone said nothing, and his face did not change as they advanced.

"Don't you see?" cried the young girl. "Can't you do anything? Can't you stop him?"

"Oh yes. I think I can do that," answered Brook indifferently. "It is rather rough on the mule."

"Rough! It's brutal, it's beastly, it's cowardly, it's perfectly inhuman!"

At that moment the unfortunate animal stumbled, struggled to recover itself as the lash descended pitilessly upon its thin flanks, and then fell headlong and tumbled upon its side. The heavy cart pulled back, half turning, so that the shafts were dragged sideways across the mule, whose weight prevented the load from rolling down hill. The carrier stopped singing and swore, beating the beast with all his might, as it lay still gasping for breath.

"Ah, assassin! Ah, carrion! I will teach thee! Curses on the dead of thy house!" he roared.

Brook and Clare were coming nearer.

"That's not very intelligent of the fellow," observed Johnstone indifferently. "He had much better get down."

"Oh, stop it, stop it!" cried the young girl, suffering acutely for the helpless creature.

But the man had apparently recognised the impossibility of producing any impression unless he descended from his perch. He threw the whip to the ground and slid off the sacks. He stood looking at the mule for a moment, and then kicked it in the back with all his might. Then, just as Johnstone and Clare came up, he went round to the back of the cart, walking unsteadily, for he was evidently drunk. The two stopped by the parapet and looked on.

"He's going to unload," said Johnstone. "That's sensible, at all events."

The sacks, as usual in Italy, were bound to the cart by cords, which were fast in front, but which wound upon a heavy spindle at the back. The spindle had three holes in it, in which staves were thrust as levers, to turn it and hold the ropes taut. Two of the staves were tightly pressed against the load, while the third stood nearly upright in its hole.

The man took the third stave, a bar of elm four feet long and as thick as a man's wrist, and came round to the mule again on the side away from Clare and Johnstone. He lifted the weapon high in air, and almost before they realised what horror he was perpetrating he had struck three or four tremendous blows upon the creature's back, making as many bleeding wounds. The mule kicked and shivered violently, and its eyes were almost starting from its head.

Johnstone came up first, caught the stave in air as it was about to descend again, wrenched

it out of the man's hands, and hurled it over
Clare's head, across the parapet and into the
sea.   The man fell back a step, and his face grew
purple with rage.   He roared out a volley of
horrible oaths, in a dialect perfectly incompre-
hensible even to Clare, who knew Italian well.

"You needn't yell like that, my good man,"
said Johnstone, smiling at him.

The man was big and strong, and drunk.   He
clenched his fists, and made for his adversary,
head down, in the futile Italian fashion.   The
Englishman stepped aside, landed a left-handed
blow behind his ear, and followed it up with a
tremendous kick, which sent the fellow upon
his face in the ditch under the rocks.   Clare
looked on, and her eyes brightened singularly,
for she had fighting blood in her veins.   The
man seemed stunned, and lay still where he had
fallen.   Johnstone turned to the fallen mule,
which lay bleeding and gasping under the shafts,
and he began to unbuckle the harness.

"Could you put a big stone behind the wheel?"
he asked, as Clare tried to help him.

He knew that the cart must roll back if it
were not blocked, for he had noticed how it
stood.   Clare looked about for a stone, picked
one up by the roadside, and went to the back of
the cart, while Johnstone patted the mule's head,
and busied himself with the buckles of the har-

She sprang with all her might, threw her arms round the drunken man's neck from behind, and dragged him backward. — *Page* 137.

ness, bending low as he did so. Clare also bent down, trying to force the stone under the wheel, and did not notice that the carter was sitting up by the roadside, feeling for something in his pocket.

An instant later he was on his feet. When Clare stood up, he was stepping softly up behind Johnstone. As he moved, she saw that he had an open clasp-knife in his right hand. Johnstone was still bending down unconscious of his danger. The young girl was light on her feet and quick, and not cowardly. The man was before her, halfway between her and Brook. She sprang with all her might, threw her arms round the drunken man's neck from behind, and dragged him backward. He struck wildly behind him with the knife, and roared out curses.

" Quick ! " cried Clare, in her high, clear voice. " He's got a knife ! Quick ! "

But Johnstone had heard their steps, and was already upon him from before, while the young girl's arms tightened round his neck from behind. The fellow struck about him wildly with his blade, staggering backwards as Clare dragged upon him.

" Let go, or you'll fall ! " Brook shouted to her.

As he spoke, dodging the knife, he struck the man twice in the face, left and right, in an earnest, business-like way. Clare caught herself by the wheel of the cart as she sprang aside, almost falling under the man's weight. A moment later, Brook was kneeling on his chest, having the knife in his hand and holding it near the carter's throat.

"Lie still!" he said rather quietly, in English. "Give me the halter, please!" he said to Clare, without looking up. "It's hanging to the shaft there in a coil."

Kneeling on the man's chest — to tell the truth, he was badly stunned, though not unconscious — Brook took two half-hitches with the halter round one wrist, passed the line under his neck as he lay, and hauled on it till the arm came under his side, then hitched the other wrist, passed the line back, hauled on it, and finally took two turns round the throat. Clare watched the operation, very pale and breathing hard.

"He's drunk," observed Johnstone. "Otherwise I wouldn't tie him up, you know. Now, if you move," he said in English to his prisoner, "you'll strangle yourself."

Thereupon he rose, forced the fellow to roll over, and hitched the fall of the line round both wrists again, and made it fast, so that the man lay, with his head drawn back by his own hands, which he could not move without tightening the rope round his neck.

"He's frightened now," said Brook. "Let's get the poor mule out of that."

In a few minutes he got the wretched beast free. It was ready enough to rise as soon as it felt that it could do so, and it struggled to its feet, badly hurt by the beating and bleeding in many places, but not seriously injured. The carter watched them as he lay on the road, half strangled, and cursed them in a choking voice.

"And now, what in the world are we going to do with them?" asked Brook, rubbing the mule's nose. "It's a pretty bad case," he continued, thoughtfully. "The mule can't draw the load, the carter can't be allowed to beat the mule, and we can't afford to let the carter have his head. What the dickens are we to do?"

He laughed a little. Then he suddenly looked hard at Clare, as though remembering something.

"It was awfully plucky of you to jump on him in that way," he said. "Just at the right moment, too, by Jove! That devil would have got at me if you hadn't stopped him. Awfully plucky, upon my word! And I'm tremendously obliged, Miss Bowring, indeed I am!"

"It's nothing to be grateful for, it seems to me," Clare answered. "I suppose there's nothing to be done but to sit down and wait until somebody comes. It's a lonely road, of course, and we may wait a long time."

"I say," exclaimed Johnstone, "you've torn your frock rather badly! Look at it!"

She drew her skirt round with her hand. There were long, clean rents in the skirt, on her right side.

"It was his knife," she said, thoughtfully surveying the damage. "He kept trying to get at me with it. I'm sorry, for I haven't another serge skirt with me."

Then she felt herself blushing, and turned away.

"I'll just pin it up," she said, and she disappeared behind the cart rather precipitately.

"By Jove! You have pretty good nerves!" observed Johnstone, more to himself than to her. "Shut up!" he cried to the carter, who was swearing again. "Stop that noise, will you?"

He made a step angrily towards the man, for the sight of the slit frock had roused him again, when he thought what the knife might have done. The fellow was silent instantly, and lay quite still, for he knew that he should strangle himself if he moved.

"I'll have you in prison before night," continued Johnstone, speaking English to him. "Oh yes! the *carabinieri* will come, and you will go to *galera* — do you understand that?"

He had picked up the words somewhere. The man began to moan and pray.

"Stop that noise!" cried Brook, with slow emphasis.

He was not far wrong in saying that the carabineers would come. They patrol the roads day and night, in pairs, as they patrol every high road and every mountain path in Italy, all the year round. And just then, far up the road down which Johnstone and Clare had come, two of them appeared in sight, recognisable a mile away by their snow-white crossbelts and gleaming accoutrements. There are twelve or fourteen thousand of them in the country, trained soldiers and picked men, by all odds the finest corps in the army. Until lately no man could serve in the carabineers who could not show documentary evidence that neither he nor his father nor his mother had ever been in prison even for the smallest offence. They are feared and respected, and it is they who have so greatly reduced brigandage throughout the country.

Clare came back to Johnstone's side, having done what she could to pin the rents together.

"It's all right now," she cried. "Here come the carabineers. They will take the man and his cart to the next village. Let me talk to them — I can speak Italian, you know."

She was pale again, and very quiet. She had

noticed that her hands trembled violently when she was pinning her frock, though they had been steady enough when they had gone round the man's throat.

When the patrol men came up, she stepped forward and explained what had happened, clearly and briefly. There was the bleeding mule, Johnstone standing before it and rubbing its dusty nose; there was the knife; there was the man. With a modest gesture she showed them where her frock had been cut to shreds. Johnstone made remarks in English, reflecting upon the Italian character, which she did not think fit to translate.

The carabineers were silent fellows with big moustaches — the one very dark, the other as fair as a Swede — they were clean, strong, sober men, with frank eyes, and they said very little. They asked the strangers' names, and Johnstone, at Clare's request, wrote her name on his card, and the address in Amalfi. One of them knew the carter for a bad character.

"We will take care of him and his cart," said the dark man, who was the superior. "The signori may go in quiet."

They untied the rope that bound the man. He rose trembling, and stood on his feet, for he knew that he was in their power. But they showed no intention of putting him in handcuffs.

" Turn the cart round ! " said the dark man.

They helped the carter to do it, and blocked it with stones.

" Put in the mule ! " was the next order, and the carabineers held up the shafts while the man obeyed.

Then both saluted Johnstone and Clare, and shouldered their short carbines, which had stood against the parapet.

" Forward ! " said the dark man, quietly.

The carter took the mule by the head and started it gently enough. The creature understood, and was glad to go down hill; the wheels creaked, the cart moved, and the party went off, one of the carabineers marching on either side.

Clare drew a long breath as she stood looking after them for a moment.

"Let us go home," she said at last, and turned up the road.

For some minutes they walked on in silence.

" I think you probably saved my life at the risk of yours, Miss Bowring," said Johnstone, at last, looking up. " Thank you very much."

" Nonsense ! " exclaimed the young girl, and she tried to laugh.

" But you were telling me that you were not combative — that you always avoided a fight, you know, and that you were so mild, and all that. For a very mild man, Mr. Johnstone, who hates fighting, you are a good 'man of your hands,' as they say in the *Morte d'Arthur*."

" Oh, I don't call that a fight ! " answered Johnstone, contemptuously. "Why, my collar isn't even crumpled. As for my hands, if I could find a spring I would wash them, after touching that fellow."

"That's the advantage of wearing gloves," observed Clare, looking at her own.

They were both very young, and though they knew that they had been in great danger they affected perfect indifference about it to each other, after the manner of true Britons. But each admired the other, and Brook was suddenly conscious that he had never known a woman whom, in some ways, he thought so admirable as Clare Bowring, but both felt a singular constraint as they walked homeward.

" Do you know ? " Clare began, when they were near Amalfi, " I think we had better say nothing about it to my mother — that is, if you don't mind."

" By all means," answered Brook. "I'm sure I don't want to talk about it."

" No, and my mother is very nervous — you know — about my going off to walk without her. Oh, not about you — with anybody. You see, I'd been very ill before I came here."

CHAPTER VIII

In obedience to Clare's expressed wish, Johnstone made no mention that evening of the rather serious adventure on the Salerno road. They had fallen into the habit of shaking hands when they bade each other good-night. When it was time, and the two ladies rose to withdraw, Johnstone suddenly wished that Clare would make some little sign to him — the least thing to show that this particular evening was not precisely what all the other evenings had been, that they were drawn a little closer together, that perhaps she would change her mind and not dislike him any more for that unknown reason at which he could not even guess.

They joined hands, and his eyes met hers. But there was no unusual pressure — no little acknowledgment of a common danger past. The blue eyes looked at him straight and proudly, without softening, and the fresh lips calmly said good-night. Johnstone remained alone, and in a singularly bad humour for such a good-tempered man. He was angry with Clare for being so cold and indifferent, and he was ashamed of himself for wishing that she would admire him a little for having knocked down a tipsy carter. It was not much of an exploit. What she had done had been very much more remarkable. The man would not have killed him, of course, but he might have given him a very dangerous wound with that ugly clasp-knife. Clare's frock was cut to pieces on one side, and it was a wonder that she had escaped without a scratch. He had no right to expect any praise for what he had done, when she had done so much more.

To tell the truth, it was not praise that he wanted, but a sign that she was not indifferent to him, or at least that she no longer disliked him. He was ashamed to own to himself that he was half in love with a young girl who had told him that she did not like him and would never even be his friend. Women had not usually treated him in that way, so far. But the fact remained, that she had got possession of his thoughts, and made him think about his actions when she was present. It took a good deal to disturb Brook Johnstone's young sleep, but he did not sleep well that night.

As for Clare, when she was alone, she regretted that she had not just nodded kindly to him, and nothing more, when she had said good-night. She knew perfectly well that he expected something of the sort, and that it would have been natural, and quite harmless, without any possibility of consequence. She consoled herself by repeating that she had done quite right, as the vision of Lady Fan rose distinctly before her in a flood of memory's moonlight. Then it struck her, as the vision faded, that her position was a very odd one. Personally, she liked the man. Impersonally, she hated and despised him. At least she believed that she did, and that she should, for the sake of all women. To her, as she had known him, he was brave, kind, gentle in manner and speech, boyishly frank. As she had seen him that once, she had thought him heartless, cowardly, and cynical. She could not reconcile the two, and therefore, in her thoughts, she unconsciously divided him into two individualities — her Mr. Johnstone and Lady Fan's Brook. There was very little resemblance between them. Oddly enough, she felt a sort of pang for him, that he could ever have been the other man whom she had first seen. She was getting into a very complicated frame of mind.

They met in the morning and exchanged greetings with unusual coldness. Brook asked whether she were tired; she said that she had done nothing to tire her, as though she resented the question; he said nothing in answer, and they both looked at the sea and thought it extremely dull. Presently Johnstone went off for a walk alone, and Clare buried herself in a book for the morning. She did not wish to think, because her thoughts were so very contradictory. It was easier to try and follow some one else's ideas. She found that almost worse than thinking, but, being very tenacious, she stuck to it and tried to read.

At the midday meal they exchanged commonplaces, and neither looked at the other. Just as they left the dining-room a heavy thunderstorm broke overhead with a deluge of rain. Clare said that the thunder made her head ache, and she disappeared on pretence of lying down. Mrs. Bowring went to write letters, and Johnstone hung about the reading-room, and smoked a pipe in the long corridor, till he was sick of the sound of his own footsteps. Amalfi was all very well in fine weather, he reflected, but when it rained it was as dismal as penny whist, Sunday in London, or a volume of sermons — or all three together, he added viciously, in his thoughts. The German family had fallen back upon the guide book, Mommsen's *History of Rome*, and the *Gartenlaube*. The Russian invalid was presumably in his room, with a teapot, and the two English old maids were reading a violently sensational novel aloud to each other by turns in the hotel drawing-room. They

Johnstone hung about the reading-room, and smoked a pipe in the long corridor, till he was sick of the sound of his own footsteps.

— *Page* 148.

stopped reading and got very red, when Johnstone looked in.

It was a dreary afternoon, and he wished that
something would happen. The fight on the preceding day had stirred his blood — and other
things perhaps had contributed to his restless
state of mind. He thought of Clare's torn
frock, and he wished he had killed the carter
outright. He reflected that, as the man was
attacking him with a knife, he himself would
have been acquitted.

Late in the afternoon the sky cleared and the
red light of the lowering sun struck the crests
of the higher hills to eastward. Brook went
out and smelled the earth-scented air, and the
damp odour of the orange-blossoms. But that
did not please him either, so he turned back
and went through the long corridor to the platform at the back of the hotel. To his surprise
he came face to face with Clare, who was walking briskly backwards and forwards, and saw
him just as he emerged from the door. They
both stood still and looked at each other with
an odd little constraint, almost like anxiety,
in their faces. There was a short, awkward
silence.

"Well?" said Clare, interrogatively, and raising her eyebrows a very little, as though wondering why he did not speak.

"Nothing," Johnstone answered, turning his face seaward. "I wasn't going to say anything."

"Oh!—you looked as though you were."

"No," he said. "I came out to get a breath of air, that's all."

"So did I. I—I think I've been out long enough. I'll go in." And she made a step towards the door.

"Oh, please, don't!" he cried suddenly. "Can't we walk together a little bit? That is, if you are not tired."

"Oh no! I'm not tired," answered the young girl with a cold little laugh. "I'll stay if you like—just a few minutes."

"Thanks, awfully," said Brook in a shy, jerky way.

They began to walk up and down, much less quickly than Clare had been walking when alone. They seemed to have nothing to say to each other. Johnstone remarked that he thought it would not rain again just then, and after some minutes of reflection Clare said that she remembered having seen two thunderstorms within an hour, with a clear sky between, not long ago. Johnstone also thought the matter over for some time before he answered, and then said that he supposed the clouds must have been somewhere in the meantime—an observation which did not strike either Clare or even himself as particularly intelligent.

"I don't think you know much about thunderstorms," said Clare, after another silence.

"I? No — why should I?"

"I don't know. It's supposed to be just as well to know about things, isn't it?"

"I dare say," answered Brook, indifferently. "But science isn't exactly in my line, if I have any line."

They recrossed the platform in silence.

"What is your line — if you have any?" Clare asked, looking at the ground as she walked, and perfectly indifferent as to his answer.

"It ought to be beer," answered Brook, gravely. "But then, you know how it is — one has all sorts of experts, and one ends by taking their word for granted about it. I don't believe I have any line — unless it's in the way of out-of-door things. I'm fond of shooting, and I can ride fairly, you know, like anybody else."

"Yes," said Clare, "you were telling me so the other day, you know."

"Yes," Johnstone murmured thoughtfully, "that's true. Please excuse me. I'm always repeating myself."

"I didn't mean that." Her tone changed a

little. "You can be very amusing when you like, you know."

"Thanks, awfully. I should like to be amusing now, for instance, but I can't."

"Now? Why now?"

"Because I'm boring you to madness, little by little, and I'm awfully sorry too, for I want you to like me — though you say you never will — and of course you can't like a bore, can you? I say, Miss Bowring, don't you think we could strike some sort of friendly agreement — to be friends without 'liking,' somehow? I'm beginning to hate the word. I believe it's the colour of my hair or my coat — or something — that you dislike so. I wish you'd tell me. It would be much kinder. I'd go to work and change it —"

"Dye your hair?" Clare laughed, glad that the ice was broken again.

"Oh yes — if you like," he answered, laughing too. "Anything to please you."

"Anything 'in reason' — as you proposed yesterday."

"No — anything in reason or out of it. I'm getting desperate!" He laughed again, but in his laughter there was a little note of something new to the young girl, a sort of understreak of earnestness.

"It isn't anything you can change," said

Clare, after a moment's hesitation. "And it certainly has nothing to do with your appearance, or your manners, or your tailor," she added.

"Oh well, then, it's evidently something I've done, or said," Brook murmured, looking at her.

But she did not return his glance, as they walked side by side; indeed, she turned her face from him a little, and she said nothing, for she was far too truthful to deny his assertion.

"Then I'm right," he said, with an interrogation, after a long pause.

"Don't ask me, please! It's of no importance after all. Talk of something else."

"I don't agree with you," Brook answered. "It is very important to me."

"Oh, nonsense!" Clare tried to laugh. "What difference can it make to you, whether I like you or not?"

"Don't say that. It makes a great difference — more than I thought it could, in fact. One — one doesn't like to be misjudged by one's friends, you know."

"But I'm not your friend."

"I want you to be."

"I can't."

"You won't," said Brook, in a lower tone, and almost angrily. "You've made up your mind against me, on account of something

you've guessed at, and you won't tell me what
it is, so I can't possibly defend myself. I haven't
the least idea what it can be. I never did anything particularly bad, I believe, and I never
did anything I should be ashamed of owning.
I don't like to say that sort of thing, you know,
about myself, but you drive me to it. It isn't
fair. Upon my word, it's not fair play. You
tell a man he's a bad lot, like that, in the air,
and then you refuse to say why you think so.
Or else the whole thing is a sort of joke you've
invented — if it is, it's awfully one-sided, it
seems to me."

"Do you really think me capable of anything
so silly?" asked Clare.

"No, I don't. That makes it all the worse,
because it proves that you have — or think you
have — something against me. I don't know
much about law, but it strikes me as something
tremendously like libel. Don't you think so
yourself?"

"Oh no! Indeed I don't. Libel means saying things against people, doesn't it? I haven't
done that —"

"Indeed you have! I mean, I beg your pardon
for contradicting you like that —"

"Rather flatly," observed Clare, as they turned
in their walk, and their eyes met.

"Well, I'm sorry, but since we are talking

about it, I've got to say what I think. After all, I'm the person attacked. I have a right to defend myself."

" I haven't attacked you," answered the young girl, gravely.

" I won't be rude, if I can help it," said Brook, half roughly. " But I asked you if you disliked me for something I had done or said, and you couldn't deny it. That means that I have done or said something bad enough to make you say that you will never be my friend — and that must be something very bad indeed."

"Then you think I'm not squeamish? It would have to be something very, very bad."

" Yes."

" Thank you. Well, I thought it very bad. Anybody would, I should fancy."

" I never did anything very, very bad, so you must be mistaken," answered Johnstone, exasperated.

Clare said nothing, but walked along with her head rather high, looking straight before her. It had all happened before her eyes, on the very ground under her feet, on that platform. Johnstone knew that he had spoken roughly.

" I say," he began, " was I rude? I'm awfully sorry." Clare stopped and stood still.

" Mr. Johnstone, we sha'n't agree. I will

never tell you, and you will never be satisfied unless I do.   So it's a dead-lock."

"You are horribly unjust," answered Brook, very much in earnest, and fixing his bright eyes on hers.   "You seem to take a delight in tormenting me with this imaginary secret.   After all, if it's something you saw me do, or heard me say, I must know of it and remember it, so there's no earthly reason why we shouldn't discuss it."

There was again that fascination in his eyes, and she felt herself yielding.

"I'll say one thing," she said.   "I wish you hadn't done it!"

She felt that she could not look away from him, and that he was getting her into his power. The colour rose in her face.

"Please don't look at me!" she said suddenly, gazing helplessly into his eyes, but his steady look did not change.

"Please — oh, please look away!" she cried, half-frightened and growing pale again.

He turned from her, surprised at her manner.

"I'm afraid you're not in earnest about this, after all," he said, thoughtfully.   "If you meant what you said, why shouldn't you look at me?"

She blushed scarlet again.

"It's very rude to stare like that!" she said,

in an offended tone. "You know that you've got something — I don't know what to call it — one can't look away when you look at one. Of course you know it, and you ought not to do it. It isn't nice."

"I didn't know there was anything peculiar about my eyes," said Brook. "Indeed I didn't! Nobody ever told me so, I'm sure. By Jove!" he exclaimed, "I believe it's that! I've probably done it before — and that's why you — " he stopped.

"Please don't think me so silly," answered Clare, recovering her composure. "It's nothing of the sort. As for that — that way you have of looking — I dare say I'm nervous since my illness. Besides — " she hesitated, and then smiled. "Besides, do you know? If you had looked at me a moment longer I should have told you the whole thing, and then we should both have been sorry."

"I should not, I'm sure," said Brook, with conviction. "But I don't understand about my looking at you. I never tried to mesmerise any one — "

"There is no such thing as mesmerism. It's all hypnotism, you know."

"I don't know what they call it. You know what I mean. But I'm sure it's your imagination."

"Oh yes, I dare say," answered the young girl with affected carelessness. "It's merely because I'm nervous."

"Well, so far as I'm concerned, it's quite unconscious. I don't know — I suppose I wanted to see in your eyes what you were thinking about. Besides, when one likes a person, one doesn't think it so dreadfully rude to look at them — at him — I mean, at you — when one is in earnest about something — does one?"

"I don't know," said Clare. "But please don't do it to me. It makes me feel awfully uncomfortable somehow. You won't, will you?" she asked, with a sort of appeal. "You would make me tell you everything — and then I should hate myself."

"But I shouldn't hate you."

"Oh yes, you would! You would hate me for knowing."

"By Jove! It's too bad!" cried Brook. "But as for that," he added humbly, "nothing would make me hate you."

"Nothing? You don't know!"

"Yes, I do! You couldn't make me change my mind about you. I've grown to — to like you a great deal too much for that in this short time — a great deal more than is good for me, I believe," he added, with a sort of rough impulsiveness. "Not that I'm at all surprised, you

A silence followed. The warm blood mantled softly in the girl's
fair cheeks. — *Page* 159.

know," he continued with an attempt at a laugh. "One can't see a person like you, most of the day, for ten days or a fortnight, without — well, you know, admiring you most tremendously — can one? I dare say you think that might be put into better English. But it's true all the same."

A silence followed. The warm blood mantled softly in the girl's fair cheeks. She was taken by surprise with an odd little breath of happiness, as it were, suddenly blowing upon her, whence she knew not. It was so utterly new that she wondered at it, and was not conscious of the faint blush that answered it.

"One gets awfully intimate in a few days," observed Brook, as though he had discovered something quite new.

She nodded, but said nothing, and they still walked up and down. Then his words made her think of that sudden intimacy which had probably sprung up between him and Lady Fan on board the yacht, and her heart was hardened again.

"It isn't worth while to be intimate, as you call it," she said at last, with a little sudden sharpness. "People ought never to be intimate, unless they have to live together — in the same place, you know. Then they can't exactly help it, I suppose."

"Why should they? One can't exactly intrench oneself behind a wall with pistols and say 'Be my friend if you dare.' Life would be very uncomfortable, I should think."

"Oh, you know what I mean! Don't be so awfully literal."

"I was trying to understand," said Johnstone, with unusual meekness. "I won't, if you don't want me to. But I don't agree with you a bit. I think it's very jolly to be intimate — in this sort of way — or perhaps a little more so."

"Intimate enemies? Enemies can be just as intimate as friends, you know."

"I'd rather have you for my intimate enemy than not know you at all," said Brook.

"That's saying a great deal, Mr. Johnstone."

Again she was pleased in a new way by what he said. And a temptation came upon her unawares. It was perfectly clear that he was beginning to make love to her. She thought of her reflections after she had seen him alone with Lady Fan, and of how she had wished that she could break his heart, and pay him back with suffering for the pain he had given another woman. The possibility seemed nearer now than then. At least, she could easily let him believe that she believed him, and then laugh at him and his acting. For of course it was acting. How could such a man be earnest? All at once the thought that he should respect her so little as to pretend to make love to her incensed her.

"What an extraordinary idea!" she exclaimed rather scornfully. "You would rather be hated, than not known!"

"I wasn't talking generalities — I was speaking of you. Please don't misunderstand me on purpose. It isn't kind."

"Are you in need of kindness just now? You don't exactly strike one in that way, you know. But your people will be coming in a day or two, I suppose. I've no doubt they'll be kind to you, as you call it — whatever that may mean. One speaks of being kind to animals and servants, you know — that sort of thing."

Nothing can outdo the brutality of a perfectly unaffected young girl under certain circumstances.

"I don't class myself with either, thank you," said Brook, justly offended. "You certainly manage to put things in a new light sometimes. I feel rather like that mule we saw yesterday."

"Oh — I thought you didn't class yourself with animals!" she laughed.

"Have you any particular reason for saying horridly disagreeable things?" asked Brook coldly.

There was a pause.

"I didn't mean to be disagreeable — at least

M

not so disagreeable as all that," said Clare at
last. "I don't know why it is, but you have a
talent for making me seem rude."

"Force of example," suggested Johnstone.

"No, I'll say that for you — you have very
good manners."

"Thanks, awfully. Considering the provoca-
tion, you know, that's an immense compliment."

"I thought I would be 'kind' for a change.
By the bye, what are we quarrelling about?"
She laughed. "You began by saying something
very nice to me, and then I told you that you
were like the mule, didn't I? It's very odd!
I believe you hypnotise me, after all."

"At all events, if we were not intimate, you
couldn't possibly say the things you do," observed Brook, already pacified.

"And I suppose you would not take the
things I say, so meekly, would you?"

"I told you I was a very mild person," said
Johnstone. "We were talking about it yesterday, do you remember?"

"Oh yes! And then you illustrated your
idea of meekness by knocking down the first
man we met."

"It was your fault," retorted Brook. "You
told me to stop his beating the mule. So I did.
Fortunately you stopped him from sticking a
knife into me. Do you know? You have

awfully good nerves. Most women would have screamed and run up a tree — or something. They would have got out of the way, at all events."

"I think most women would have done precisely what I did," said Clare. "Why should you say that most women are cowards?"

"I didn't," answered Brook. "But I refuse to quarrel about it. I meant to say that I admired you — I mean, what you did — well, more than anything."

"That's a sweeping sort of compliment. Am I to return it?" She glanced at him and smiled.

"You couldn't, with truth."

"Of course I could. I don't remember ever seeing anything of that sort before, but I don't believe that anybody could have done it better. I admired you more than anything just then, you know." She laughed once more as she added the last words.

"Oh, I don't expect you to go on admiring me. I'm quite satisfied, and grateful, and all that."

"I'm glad you're so easily satisfied. Couldn't we talk seriously about something or other? It seems to me that we've been chaffing for half an hour, haven't we?"

"It hasn't been all chaff, Miss Bowring," said Johnstone. "At least, not on my side."

"Then I'm sorry," Clare answered. They relapsed into silence, as they walked their beat, to and fro. The sun had gone down, and it was already twilight on that side of the mountains. The rain had cooled the air, and the far land to southward was darkly distinct beyond the purple water. It was very chilly, and Clare was without a shawl, and Johnstone was hatless, but neither of them noticed that it was cool. Johnstone was the first to speak.

"Is this sort of thing to go on for ever, Miss Bowring?" he asked gravely.

"What?" But she knew very well what he meant.

"This — this very odd footing we are on, you and I — are we never going to get past it?"

"Oh — I hope not," answered Clare, cheerfully. "I think it's very pleasant, don't you? And most original. We are intimate enough to say all sorts of things, and I'm your enemy, and you say you are my friend. I can't imagine any better arrangement. We shall always laugh when we think of it — even years hence. You will be going away in a few days, and we shall stay here into the summer and we shall never see each other again, in all probability. We shall always look back on this time — as something quite odd, you know."

" You are quite mistaken if you think that we shall never meet again," said Johnstone.

" I mean that it's very unlikely. You see we don't go home very often, and when we do we stop with friends in the country. We don't go much into society. And the rest of the time we generally live in Florence."

" There is nothing to prevent me from coming to Florence — or living there, if I choose."

" Oh no — I suppose not. Except that you would be bored to death. It's not very amusing, unless you happen to be fond of pictures, and you never said you were."

" I should go to see you."

" Oh — yes — you could call, and of course if we were at home we should be very glad to see you. But that would only occupy about half an hour of one day. That isn't much."

" I mean that I should go to Florence simply for the sake of seeing you, and seeing you often — all the time, in fact."

" Dear me! That would be a great deal, wouldn't it? I thought you meant just to call, don't you know? "

" I'm in earnest, though it sounds very funny, I dare say," said Johnstone.

" It sounds rather mad," answered Clare, laughing a little. " I hope you won't do anything of the kind, because I wouldn't see you

more than once or twice. I'd have headaches
and colds and concerts — all the things one has
when one isn't at home to people. But my
mother would be delighted. She likes you tremendously, you know, and you could go about
to galleries together and read Ruskin and Browning — do you know the Statue and the Bust?
And you could go and see Casa Guidi, where the
Brownings lived, and you could drive up to San
Miniato, and then, you know, you could drive
up again and read more Browning and more
Ruskin. I'm sure you would enjoy it to any
extent. But I should have to go through a ter-
rific siege of colds and headaches. It would be
rather hard on me."

"And harder on me," observed Brook, "and
quite fearful for Mrs. Bowring."

"Oh no! She would enjoy every minute of it.
You forget that she likes you."

"You are afraid I should forget that you
don't."

"I almost — oh, a long way from quite! I
almost liked you yesterday when you thrashed
the carter and tied him up so neatly. It was
beautifully done — all those knots! I suppose
you learned them on board of the yacht, didn't
you?"

"I've yachted a good deal," said Brook.

"Generally with that party?" inquired Clare.

"No. That was the first time. My father has an old tub he goes about in, and we sometimes go together."

" Is he coming here in his 'old tub'?"

" Oh no — he's lent her to a fellow who has taken her off to Japan, I believe."

"Japan! Is it safe? In an 'old tub'!"

"Oh, well — that's a way of talking, you know. She's a good enough boat, you know. My father went to New York in her, last year. She's a steamer, you know. I hate steamers. They are such dirty noisy things! But of course if you are going a long way, they are the only things."

He spoke in a jerky way, annoyed and discomfited by her forcing the conversation off the track. Though he was aware that he had gone further than he intended, when he proposed to spend the winter in Florence. Moreover, he was very tenacious by nature, and had rarely been seriously opposed during his short life. Her persistent refusal to tell him the cause of her deep-rooted dislike exasperated him, while her frank and careless manner and good-fellowship fascinated him more and more.

" Tell me all about the yacht," she said. " I'm sure she is a beauty, though you call her an old tub."

" I don't want to talk about yachts," he an-

swered, returning to the attack in spite of her.
" I want to talk about the chances of seeing you
after we part here."

" There aren't any," replied the young girl
carelessly.   " What is the name of the yacht?"

" Very commonplace — ' Lucy,' that's all.   I'll
make chances if there are none —"

" You mustn't say that ' Lucy ' is commonplace.   That's my mother's name."

"I beg your pardon.   I couldn't know that.
It always struck me that it wasn't much of a
name for a yacht, you know.   That was all I
meant.   He's a queer old bird, my father; he
always says he took it from the Bride of Lam-
mermoor, Heaven knows why.   But please — I
really can't go away and feel that I'm not to see
you again soon.   You seem to think that I'm
chaffing.   I'm not.   I'm very serious.   I like
you very much, and I don't see why one should
just meet and then go off, and let that be the
end — do you?"

" I don't see why not," exclaimed Clare, hating
the unexpected longing she felt to agree with
him, and tell him to come and stay in Florence
as much as he pleased.   " Come — it's too cold
here.   I must be going in."

CHAPTER IX

BROOK JOHNSTONE had never been in the habit of observing his sensations nor of paying any great attention to his actions. He was not at all an actor, as Clare believed him to be, and the idea that he could ever have taken pleasure in giving pain would have made him laugh. Possibly, it would have made him very angry, but it certainly had no foundation at all in fact. He had been liked, loved, and made much of, not for anything he had ever taken the trouble to do, but partly for his own sake, and partly on account of his position. Such charm as he had for women lay in his frankness, good humour, and simplicity of character. That he had appeared to be changeable in his affection was merely due to the fact that he had never been in love. He vaguely recognised the fact in his inner consciousness, though he would have said that he had been in love half a dozen times ; which only amounted to saying that women he had liked had been in love with him or had thought that they were, or had wished to have it thought that he loved them or had perhaps, like poor Lady Fan, been willing to risk a good deal on the bare chance of marrying one of the best of society's matches in the end. He was too young to look upon such affairs very seriously. When he had been tired of the game he had not lacked the courage to say so, and in most cases he had been forgiven. Lady Fan might prove an exception, but he hoped not. He was enormously far removed from being a saint, it is true, but it is due to him to repeat that he had drawn the line rigidly at a certain limit, and that all women beyond that line had been to him as his own mother, in thought and deed. Let those who have the right to cast stones — and the cruelty to do so — decide for themselves whether Brook Johnstone was a bad man at heart, or not. It need not be hinted that a proportion of the stone-throwing Pharisees owe their immaculate reputation to their conspicuous lack of attraction; the little band has a place apart and they stand there and lapidate most of us, and secretly wish that they had ever had the chance of being as bad as we are without being found out. But the great army of the pure in heart are mixed with us sinners in the fight, and though they may pray for us, they do not carp at our imperfections — and occasionally they get hit by the Pharisees just as we do, being rather whiter than we and

therefore offering a more tempting mark for a
jagged stone or a handful of pious mud. You
may know the Pharisee by his intimate knowledge of the sins he has never committed.

Besides, though the code of honour is not
worth much as compared with the Ten Com-
mandments, it is notably better than nothing, in
the way of morality. It will keep a man from
lying and evil speaking as well as from picking
and stealing, and if it does not force him to honour all women as angels, it makes him respect
a very large proportion of them as good women
and therefore sacred, in a very practical way of
sacredness. Brook Johnstone always was very
careful in all matters where honour and his own
feeling about honour were concerned. For that
reason he had told Clare that he had never done
anything very bad, whereas what she had seen
him do was monstrous in her eyes. She had not
reflected that she knew nothing about Lady Fan;
and if she had heard half there was to be known
she would not have understood. That night on
the platform Lady Fan had given her own ver-
sion of what had taken place on the Acropolis
at sunset, and Brook had not denied anything.
Clare did not reflect that Lady Fan might very
possibly have exaggerated the facts very much
in her statement of them, and that at such a
time Brook was certainly not the man to argue

the case, since it had manifestly been his only course to take all the apparent blame on himself. Even if he had known that Clare had heard the conversation, he could not possibly have explained the matter to her — not even if she had been an old woman — without telling all the truth about Lady Fan, and he was too honourable a man to do that, under any conceivable circumstances.

He was decidedly and really in love with the girl. He knew it, because what he felt was not like anything he had ever felt before. It was anything but the pleasurable excitement to which he was accustomed. There might have been something of that if he had received even the smallest encouragement. But, do what he would, he could find none. The attraction increased, and the encouragement was daily less, he thought. Clare occasionally said things which made him half believe that she did not wholly dislike him. That was as much as he could say. He cudgelled his brains and wrung his memory to discover what he could have done to offend her, and he could not remember anything — which was not surprising. It was clear that she had never heard of him before he had come to Amalfi. He had satisfied himself of that by questions, otherwise he would naturally enough have come near the truth and guessed that she must have known of some affair in which he had been concerned, which she judged harshly from her own point of view.

He was beginning to suffer, and he was not accustomed to suffering, least of all to any of the mental kind, for his life had always gone smoothly. He had believed hitherto that most people exaggerated, and worried themselves unnecessarily, but when he found it hard to sleep, and noticed that he had a dull, unsatisfied sort of misery with him all day long, he began to understand. He did not think that Clare could really enjoy teasing him, and, besides, it was not like mere teasing, either. She was evidently in earnest when she repeated that she did not like him. He knew her face when she was chaffing, and her tone, and the little bending of the delicate, swan-like throat, too long for perfect beauty, but not for perfect grace. When she was in earnest, her head rose, her eyes looked straight before her, and her voice sank to a graver note. He knew all the signs of truth, for with her it was always very near the surface, dwelling not in a deep well, but in clear water, as it were, open to the sky. Her truth was evidently truth, and her jesting was transparent as a child's.

It looked a hopeless case, but he had no intention of considering it without hope, nor any inclination to relinquish his attempts. He did not tell himself in so many words that he wished to marry her, and intended to marry her, and would marry her, if it were humanly possible, and he assuredly made no such promises to himself. Nor did he look at her as he had looked at women in whom he had been momentarily interested, appreciating her good points of face and figure, cataloguing and compiling her attractions so as to admire them all in turn, forget none, and receive their whole effect.

He had a restless, hungry craving that left him no peace, and that seemed to desire only a word, a look, the slightest touch of sympathy, to be instantly satisfied. And he could not get from her one softened glance, nor one sympathetic pressure of the hand, nor one word spoken more gravely than another, except the assurance of her genuine dislike.

That was the only thing he had to complain of, but it was enough. He could not reproach her with having encouraged him, for she had told him the truth from the first. He had not quite believed her. So much the worse for him. If he had, and if he had gone to Naples to wait for his people, all this would not have happened, for he had not fallen in love at first sight. A fortnight of daily and almost hourly intercourse was very good and reasonable ground for being in love.

He grew absent-minded, and his pipe went out unexpectedly, which always irritated him, and sometimes he did not take the trouble to light it again. He rose at dawn and went for long walks in the hills, with the idea that the early air and the lofty coolness would do him good, and with the acknowledged intention of doing his walking at an hour when he could not possibly be with Clare. For he could not keep away from her, whether Mrs. Bowring were with her or not. He was too much a man of the world to sit all day long before her, glaring at her in shy silence, as a boy might have done, and as he would have been content to do; so he took immense pains to be agreeable, when her mother was present, and Mrs. Bowring liked him, and said that he had really a most extraordinary talent for conversation. It was not that he ever said anything very memorable; but he talked most of the time, and always pleasantly, telling stories about people and places he had known, discussing the lighter books of the day, and affecting that profound ignorance of politics which makes some women feel at their ease, and encourages amusing discussion.

Mrs. Bowring watched him when she was there with a persistency which might have made him nervous if he had not been wholly absorbed in her daughter. She evidently saw something

in him which reminded her of some one or something. She had changed of late, and Clare was
beginning to think that she must be ill, though
she scouted the suggestion, and said that she
was growing daily stronger. She had altogether
relaxed her vigilance with regard to the two
young people, and seemed willing that they
should go where they pleased together, and sit
alone together by the hour.

"I dare say I watched him a good deal at
first," she said to her daughter. "But I have
made up my mind about him. He's a very
good sort of young fellow, and I'm glad that
you have a companion. You see I can't walk
much, and now that you are getting better you
need exercise. After all, one can always trust
the best of one's own people. He's not falling
in love with you, is he, dear? I sometimes
fancy that he looks at you as though he were."

"Nonsense, mother!" and Clare laughed in-
tentionally. "But he's very good company."

"It would be very unfortunate if he did," said
Mrs. Bowring, looking away, and speaking almost to herself. "I am not sure that we should
not have gone away —"

"Really! If one is to be turned out of the
most beautiful place in the world because a
young Englishman chooses to stop in the same
hotel! Besides, why in the world should he

fall in love with me? He's used to a very different kind of people, I fancy."

"What do you mean?"

"Oh—the gay set—'a' gay set, I suppose, for there are probably more than one of them. They are quite different from us, you know."

"That is no reason. On the contrary—men like variety and change—change, yes," repeated Mrs. Bowring, with an odd emphasis. "At all events, child, don't take a fancy to him!" she added. "Not that I'm much afraid of that. You are anything but 'susceptible,' my dear!" she laughed faintly.

"You need not be in the least afraid," answered Clare. "But, after all, mother—just supposing the case—I can't see why it should be such an awful calamity if we took a fancy to each other. We belong to the same class of people, if not to the same set. He has enough money, and I'm not absolutely penniless, though we are as poor as church mice—"

"For Heaven's sake, don't suggest such a thing!" cried Mrs. Bowring.

Her face was white, and her lips trembled. There was a frightened look in her pale eyes, and she turned her face quickly to her daughter, and quickly away again.

"Mother!" exclaimed the young girl, in surprise. "What in the world is the matter? I

was only laughing — besides — " she stopped,
puzzled. " Tell me the truth, mother," she continued suddenly. " You know about his people —
his father is some connection of — of your first
husband — there's some disgraceful story about
them — tell me the truth. Why shouldn't I
know ? "

" I hope you never will ! " answered Mrs. Bowring, in a low voice that had a sort of horror
in it.

" Then there is something ? " Clare herself
turned a little paler as she asked the question.

"Don't ask me — don't ask me ! "

" Something disgraceful ? " The young girl
leaned forward as she spoke, and her eyes were
wide and anxious, forcing her mother to speak.

" Yes — no," faltered Mrs. Bowring. " Nothing to do with this one — something his father
did long ago."

" Dishonourable ? " asked Clare, her voice sinking lower and lower.

" No — not as men look at it — oh, don't ask
me ! Please don't ask me — please don't, darling ! "

" Then his yacht is named after you," said
the young girl in a flash of intelligence.

" His yacht ? " asked the elder woman ex-
citedly. " What ? I don't understand."

" Mr. Johnstone told me that his father had a

"Mother, sweet! of course I love you!" — *Page* 179.

big steam yacht called the 'Lucy' — mother, that man loved you, he loves you still."

" Me ? Oh no — no, he never loved me ! " She laughed wildly, with quivering lips. " Don't, child — don't ! For God's sake don't ask questions — you'll drive me mad ! It's the secret of my life — the only secret I have from you — oh, Clare, if you love me at all — don't ask me ! "

" Mother, sweet ! Of course I love you ! "

The young girl, very pale and wondering, kneeled beside the elder woman and threw her arms round her and drew down her face, kissing the white cheeks and the starting tears and the faded flaxen hair. The storm subsided, almost without breaking, for Mrs. Bowring was a brave woman and, in some ways, a strong woman, and whatever her secret might be, she had kept it long and well from her daughter.

Clare knew her, and inwardly decided that the secret must have been worth keeping. She loved her mother far too well to hurt her with questions, but she was amazed at what she herself felt of resentful curiosity to know the truth about anything which could cast a shadow upon the man she disliked, as she thought so sincerely. Her mind worked like lightning, while her voice spoke softly and her hands sought those thin, familiar, gentle fingers which were an integral part of her world and life.

Two possibilities presented themselves. Johnstone's father was a brother or near connection of her mother's first husband. Either she had loved him, been deceived in him, and had married the brother instead; or, having married, this man had hated her and fought against her, and harmed her, because she was his elder brother's wife, and he coveted the inheritance. In either case it was no fault of Brook's. The most that could be said would be that he might have his father's character. She inclined to the first of her theories. Old Johnstone had made love to her mother and had half broken her heart, before she had married his brother. Brook was no better — and she thought of Lady Fan. But she was strangely glad that her mother had said "not dishonourable, as men look at it." It had been as though a cruel hand had been taken from her throat, when she had heard that.

"But, mother," she said presently, "these people are coming to-morrow or the next day — and they mean to stay, he says. Let us go away, before they come. We can come back afterwards — you don't want to meet them."

Mrs. Bowring was calm again, or appeared to be so, whatever was passing in her mind.

"I shall certainly not run away," she answered in a low, steady voice. "I will not run away and leave Adam Johnstone's son to tell his father that I was afraid to meet him, or his wife," she added, almost in a whisper. "I've been weak, sometimes, my dear —" her voice rose to its natural key again, "and I've made a mistake in life. But I won't be a coward — I don't believe I am, by nature, and if I were I wouldn't let myself be afraid now."

"It would not be fear, mother. Why should you suffer, if you are going to suffer in meeting him? We had much better go away at once. When they have all left, we can come back."

"And you would not mind going away to-morrow, and never seeing Brook Johnstone again?" asked Mrs. Bowring, quietly.

"I? No! Why should I?"

Clare meant to speak the truth, and she thought that it was the truth. But it was not. She grew a little paler a moment after the words had passed her lips, but her mother did not see the change of colour.

"I'm glad of that, at all events," said the elder woman. "But I won't go away. No — I won't," she repeated, as though spurring her own courage.

"Very well," answered the young girl. "But we can keep very much to ourselves all the time they are here, can't we? We needn't make their acquaintance — at least — " she stopped short, realising that it would be impossible to avoid knowing Brook's people if they were stopping in the same hotel.

"Their acquaintance!" Mrs. Bowring laughed bitterly at the idea.

"Oh — I forgot," said Clare. "At all events, we need not meet unnecessarily. That's what I mean, you know."

There was a short pause, during which her mother seemed to be thinking.

"I shall see him alone, for I have something to say to him," she said at last, as though she had come to a decision. "Go out, my dear," she added. "Leave me alone a little while. I shall be all right when it is time for luncheon."

Her daughter left her, but she did not go out at once. She went to her own room and sat down to think over what she had seen and heard. If she went out she should probably find Johnstone waiting for her, and she did not wish to meet him just then. It was better to be alone. She would find out why the idea of not seeing him any more had hurt her after she had spoken.

But that was not an easy matter at all. So soon as she tried to think of herself and her own feelings, she began to think of her mother. And when she endeavoured to solve the mystery and guess the secret, her thoughts flew off suddenly to Brook, and she wished that she were outside in the sunshine talking to him. And again, as the probable conversation suggested itself to her, she was glad that she was not with him, and she tried to think again. Then she forced herself to recall the scene with Lady Fan on the terrace, and she did her best to put him in the worst possible light, which in her opinion was a very bad light indeed. And his father before him — Adam — her mother had told her the name for the first time, and it struck her as an odd one — old Adam Johnstone had been a heart-breaker, and a faith-breaker, and a betrayer of women before Brook was in the world at all. Her theory held good, when she looked at it fairly, and her resentment grew apace. It was natural enough, for in her imagination she had always hated that first husband of her mother's who had come and gone before her father; and now she extended her hatred to this probable brother, and it had much more force, because the man was alive and a reality, and was soon to come and be a visible talking person. There was one good point about him and his coming. It helped her to revive her hatred of Brook and to colour it with the inheritance of some harm done to her own mother. That certainly was an advantage.

But she should be very sorry not to see Brook any more, never to hear him talk to her again, never to look into his eyes — which, all the

same, she so unreasonably dreaded. It was beyond her powers of analysis to reconcile her like
and dislike. All the little logic she had said
that it was impossible to like and dislike the
same person at the same time. She seemed to
have two hearts, and the one cried " Hate,"
while the other cried " Love." That was absurd, and altogether ridiculous, and quite con-
temptible.

There they were, however, the two hearts,
fighting it out, or at least altercating and threat-
ening to fight and hurt her. Of course " love "
meant " like " — it was a general term, well
contrasting with " hate." As for really caring,
beyond a liking for Brook Johnstone, she was
sure that it was impossible. But the liking was
strong. She exploded her difficulty at last with
the bomb of a splendidly youthful quibble. She
said to herself that she undoubtedly hated him
and despised him, and that he was certainly the
very lowest of living men for treating Lady Fan
so badly — besides being a black sinner, a point
which had less weight. And then she told herself that the cry of something in her to " like "
instead of hating was simply the expression of
what she might have felt, and should have felt,
and should have had a right to have felt, had it
not been for poor Lady Fan ; but also of something which she assuredly did not feel, never

could feel, and never meant to feel. In other words, she should have liked Brook if she had not had good cause to dislike him. She was satisfied with this explanation of her feelings, and she suddenly felt that she could go out and see him and talk to him without being inconsistent. She had forgotten to explain to herself why she wished him not to go away. She went out accordingly, and sat down on the terrace in the soft air.

She glanced up and down, but Johnstone was not to be seen anywhere, and she wished that she had not come out after all. He had probably waited some time and had then gone for a walk by himself. She thought that he might have waited just a little longer before giving it up, and she half unconsciously made up her mind to requite him by staying indoors after luncheon. She had not even brought a book or a piece of work, for she had felt quite sure that he would be walking up and down as usual, with his pipe, looking as though he owned the scenery. She half rose to go in, and then changed her mind. She would give him one more chance and count fifty, before she went away, at a good quick rate.

She began to count. At thirty-five her pace slackened. She stopped a long time at forty-five, and then went slowly to the end. But Johnstone did not come. Once again, she reluctantly decided — and she began slowly; and again she slackened speed and dragged over the last ten numbers. But he did not come.

" Oh, this is ridiculous ! " she exclaimed aloud to herself, as she rose impatiently from her seat.

She felt injured, for her mother had sent her away, and there was no one to talk to her, and she did not care to think any more, lest the questions she had decided should again seem open and doubtful. She went into the hotel and walked down the corridor. He might be in the reading-room. She walked quickly, because she was a little ashamed of looking for him when she felt that he should be looking for her. Suddenly she stopped, for she heard him whistling somewhere. Whistling was his solitary accomplishment, and he did it very well. There was no mistaking the shakes and runs, and pretty bird-like cadences. She listened, but she bit her lip. He was light-hearted, at all events, she thought.

The sound came nearer, and Brook suddenly appeared in the corridor, his hat on the back of his head, his hands in his pockets. As he caught sight of Clare the shrill tune ceased, and one hand removed the hat.

" I've been looking for you everywhere, for the last two hours," he cried as he came along.

"Good morning," he said as he reached her. "I was just going back to the terrace in despair."

"It sounded more as though you were whistling for me," answered Clare, with a laugh, for she was instantly happy, and pacified, and peaceful.

"Well — not exactly!" he answered. "But I did hope that you would hear me and know that I was about — wishing you would come."

"I always come out in the morning," she replied with sudden demureness. "Indeed — I wondered where you were. Let us go out, shall we?"

"We might go for a walk," suggested Brook.

"It is too late."

"Just a little walk — down to the town and across the bridge to Atrani, and back. Couldn't we?"

"Oh, we could, of course. Very well — I've got a hat on, haven't I? All right. Come along!"

"My people are coming to-day," said Brook, as they passed through the door. "I've just had a telegram."

"To-day!" exclaimed Clare in surprise, and somewhat disturbed.

"Yes, you know I have been expecting them at any moment. I fancy they have been knock-

ing about, you know — seeing Pæstum and
all that. They are such queer people. They
always want to see everything — as though it
mattered!"

"There are only the two? Mr. and Mrs.
Johnstone?"

"Yes — that's all." Brook laughed a little
as though she had said something amusing.

"What are you laughing at?" asked Clare,
naturally enough.

"Oh, nothing. It's ridiculous — but it sounded
funny — unfamiliar, I mean. My father has
fallen a victim to knighthood, that's all. The
affliction came upon him some time ago, and his
name is Adam — of all the names in the world."

"It was the first," observed Clare reassur-
ingly. "It doesn't sound badly either — Sir
Adam. I beg his pardon for calling him 'Mr.'"
She laughed in her turn.

"Oh, he wouldn't mind," said Brook. "He's
not at all that sort. Do you know? I think
you'll like him awfully. He's a fine old chap
in his way, though he is a brewer. He's much
bigger than I am, but he's rather odd, you
know. Sometimes he'll talk like anything, and
sometimes he won't open his lips. We aren't
at all alike in that way. I talk all the time, I
believe — rain or shine. Don't I bore you
dreadfully sometimes?"

"No — you never bore me," answered Clare with perfect truth.

"I mean, when I talk as I did yesterday afternoon," said Johnstone with a shade of irritation.

"Oh, that — yes! Please don't begin again, and spoil our walk!"

But the walk was not destined to be a long one. A narrow, paved footway leads down from the old monastery to the shore, in zigzag, between low whitewashed walls, passing at last under some houses which are built across it on arches.

Just as they came in sight a tall old man emerged from this archway, walking steadily up the hill. He was tall and bony, with a long grey beard, shaggy bent brows, keen dark eyes, and an eagle nose. He wore clothes of rough grey woollen tweed, and carried a grey felt hat in one long hand.

A moment after he had come out of the arch he caught sight of Brook, and his rough face brightened instantly. He waved the grey hat and called out.

"Hulloa, my boy! There you are, eh!"

His voice was thin, like many Scotch voices, but it carried far, and had a manly ring in it. Brook did not answer, but waved his hat.

"That's my father," he said in a low tone to

Clare. "May I introduce him? And there's
my mother — being carried up in the chair."

A couple of lusty porters were carrying Lady
Johnstone up the steep ascent. She was a fat
lady with bright blue eyes, like her son's, and a
much brighter colour. She had a parasol in
one hand and a fan in the other, and she shook
a little with every step the porters made. In
the rear, a moment later, came other porters,
carrying boxes and bags of all sizes. Then a
short woman, evidently Lady Johnstone's maid,
came quietly along by herself, stopping occasionally to look at the sea.

Clare looked curiously at the party as they
approached. Her first impulse had been to leave
Brook and go back alone to warn her mother.
It was not far. But she realised that it would
be much better and wiser to face the introduction at once. In less than five minutes Sir
Adam had reached them. He shook hands
with Brook vigorously, and looked at him as a
man looks who loves his son. Clare saw the
glance, and it pleased her.

"Let me introduce you to Miss Bowring," said
Brook. "Mrs. Bowring and Miss Bowring are
staying here, and have been awfully good to
me."

Sir Adam turned his keen eyes to Clare, as
she held out her hand.

Sir Adam gravely introduced Clare. — *Page* 191.

"I beg your pardon," he said, "but are you a daughter of Captain Bowring who was killed some years ago in Africa?"

"Yes." She looked up to him inquiringly and distrustfully.

His face brightened again and softened — then hardened singularly, all at once. She could not have believed that such features could change so quickly.

"And my son says that your mother is here! My dear young lady — I'm very glad! I hope you mean to stay."

The words were cordial. The tone was cold. Brook stared at his father, very much surprised to find that he knew anything of the Bowrings, for he himself had not mentioned them in his letters. But the porters, walking more slowly, had just brought his mother up to where the three stood, and waited, panting a little, and the chair swinging slightly from the shoulder-straps.

"Dear old boy!" cried Lady Johnstone. "It is good to see you. No — don't kiss me, my dear — it's far too hot. Let me look at you."

Sir Adam gravely introduced Clare. Lady Johnstone's fat face became stony as a red granite mummy case, and she bent her apoplectic neck stiffly.

"Oh!" she ejaculated. "Very glad, I'm sure.

Were you going for a walk?" she asked, turning to Brook, severely.

" Yes, there was just time. I didn't know when to expect you. But if Miss Bowring doesn't mind, we'll give it up, and I'll install you. Your rooms are all ready."

It was at once clear to Clare that Lady Johnstone had never heard the name of Bowring, and that she resented the idea of her son walking alone with any young girl.

CHAPTER X

CLARE went directly to her mother's room. She had hardly spoken again during the few minutes while she had necessarily remained with the Johnstones, climbing the hill back to the hotel. At the door she had stood aside to let Lady Johnstone go in, Sir Adam had followed his wife, and Brook had lingered, doubtless hoping to exchange a few words more with Clare. But she was preoccupied, and had not vouchsafed him a glance.

"They have come," she said, as she closed Mrs. Bowring's door behind her.

Her mother was seated by the open window, her hands lying idly in her lap, her face turned away, as Clare entered. She started slightly, and looked round.

"Oh!" she exclaimed. "Already! Well — it had to come. Have you met?"

Clare told her all that had happened.

"And he said that he was glad?" asked Mrs. Bowring, with the ghost of a smile.

"He said so — yes. His voice was cold. But

when he first heard my name and asked about my father his face softened."

"His face softened," repeated Mrs. Bowring to herself, just above a whisper, as the ghost of the smile flitted about her pale lips.

" He seemed glad at first, and then he looked displeased. Is that it ? " she asked, raising her voice again.

" That was what I thought," answered Clare. "Why don't you have luncheon in your room, mother ? " she asked suddenly.

" He would think I was afraid to meet him," said the elder woman.

A long silence followed, and Clare sat down on a stiff straw chair, looking out of the window. At last she turned to her mother again.

" You couldn't tell me all about it, could you, mother dear ? " she asked. " It seems to me it would be so much easier for us both. Perhaps I could help you. And I myself — I should know better how to act."

" No. I can't tell you. I only pray that I may never have to. As for you, darling — be natural. It is a very strange position to be in, but you cannot know it — you can't be supposed to know it. I wish I could have kept my secret better — but I broke down when you told me about the yacht. You can only help me in one way — don't ask me questions, dear. It would

be harder for me, if you knew — indeed it would.
Be natural. You need not run after them, you
know —"

"I should think not!" cried Clare indignantly.

"I mean, you need not go and sit by them
and talk to them for long at a time. But don't
be suddenly cold and rude to their son. There's
nothing against — I mean, it has nothing to do
with him. You mustn't think it has, you know.
Be natural — be yourself."

"It's not altogether easy to be natural under
the circumstances," Clare answered, with some
truth, and a great deal of repressed curiosity
which she did her best to hide away altogether
for her mother's sake.

At luncheon the Johnstones were all three
placed on the opposite side of the table, and
Brook was no longer Clare's neighbour. The
Bowrings were already in their places when the
three entered, Sir Adam giving his arm to his
wife, who seemed to need help in walking, or at
all events to be glad of it. Brook followed at a
little distance, and Clare saw that he was looking at her regretfully, as though he wished himself at her side again. Had she been less young
and unconscious and thoroughly innocent, she
must have seen by this time that he was seriously in love with her.

Sir Adam held his wife's chair for her, with

somewhat old-fashioned courtesy, and pushed it gently as she sat down. Then he raised his head, and his eyes met Mrs. Bowring's. For a few moments they looked at each other. Then his expression changed and softened, as it had when he had first met Clare, but Mrs. Bowring's face grew hard and pale. He did not sit down, but to his wife's surprise walked quietly all round the end of the table and up the other side to where Mrs. Bowring sat. She knew that he was coming, and she turned a little to meet his hand. The English old maids watched the proceedings with keen interest from the upper end.

Sir Adam held out his hand, and Mrs. Bowring took it.

"It is a great pleasure to me to meet you again," he said slowly, as though speaking with an effort. "Brook says that you have been very good to him, and so I want to thank you at once. Yes — this is your daughter — Brook introduced me. Excuse me — I'll get round to my place again. Shall we meet after luncheon?"

"If you like," said Mrs. Bowring in a constrained tone. "By all means," she added nervously.

"My dear," said Sir Adam, speaking across the table to his wife, "let me introduce you to my old friend Mrs. Bowring, the mother of this young lady whom you have already met," he added, glancing down at Clare's flaxen head.

Again Lady Johnstone slightly bent her apoplectic neck, but her expression was not stony, as it had been when she had first looked at Clare. On the contrary, she smiled very pleasantly and naturally, and her frank blue eyes looked at Mrs. Bowring with a friendly interest.

Clare thought that she heard a faint sigh of relief escape her mother's lips just then. Sir Adam's heavy steps echoed upon the tile floor, as he marched all round the table again to his seat. The table itself was narrow, and it was easy to talk across it, without raising the voice. Sir Adam sat on one side of his wife, and Brook on the other, last on his side, as Clare was on hers.

There was very little conversation at first. Brook did not care to talk across to Clare, and Sir Adam seemed to have said all he meant to say for the present. Lady Johnstone, who seemed to be a cheerful, conversational soul, began to talk to Mrs. Bowring, evidently attracted by her at first sight.

"It's a beautiful place when you get here," she said. "Isn't it? The view from my window is heavenly! But to get here! Dear me! I was carried up by two men, you know, and I thought they would have died. I hope they are enjoying their dinner, poor fellows! I'm sure they never carried such a load before!"

And she laughed, with a sort of frank, half self-commiserating amusement at her own proportions.

"Oh, I fancy they must be used to it," said Mrs. Bowring, reassuringly, for the sake of saying something.

"They'll hate the sight of me in a week!" said Lady Johnstone. "I mean to go everywhere, while I'm here — up all the hills, and down all the valleys. I always see everything when I come to a new place. It's pleasant to sit still afterwards, and feel that you've done it all, don't you know? I shall ruin you in porters, Adam," she added, turning her large round face slowly to her husband.

"Certainly, certainly," answered Sir Adam, nodding gravely, as he dissected the bones out of a fried sardine.

"You're awfully good about it," said Lady Johnstone, in thanks for unlimited porters to come.

Like many unusually stout people, she ate very little, and had plenty of time for talking.

"You knew my husband a long time ago, then!" she began, again looking across at Mrs. Bowring.

Sir Adam glanced at Mrs. Bowring sharply from beneath his shaggy brows.

"Oh yes," she said calmly. "We met before he was married."

The grey-headed man slowly nodded assent, but said nothing.

"Before his first marriage?" inquired Lady Johnstone gravely. "You know that he has been married twice."

"Yes," answered Mrs. Bowring. "Before his first marriage."

Again Sir Adam nodded solemnly.

"How interesting!" exclaimed Lady Johnstone. "Such old friends! And to meet in this accidental way, in this queer place!"

"We generally live abroad," said Mrs. Bowring. "Generally in Florence. Do you know Florence?"

"Oh yes!" cried the fat lady enthusiastically. "I dote on Florence. I'm perfectly mad about pictures, you know. Perfectly mad!"

The vision of a woman cast in Lady Johnstone's proportions and perfectly mad might have provoked a smile on Mrs. Bowring's face at any other time.

"I suppose you buy pictures, as well as admire them," she said, glad of the turn the conversation had taken.

"Sometimes," answered the other. "Sometimes. I wish I could buy more. But good pictures are getting to be most frightfully dear. Besides, you are hardly ever sure of getting an original, unless there are all the documents — and that means thousands, literally thousands of pounds. But now and then I kick over the traces, you know."

Clare could not help smiling at the simile, and bent down her head. Brook was watching her, he understood and was annoyed, for he loved his mother in his own way.

" At all events you won't be able to ruin yourself in pictures here," said Mrs. Bowring.

" No — but how about the porters ? " suggested Sir Adam.

" My dear Adam," said Lady Johnstone, " unless they are all Shylocks here, they won't exact a ducat for every pound of flesh. If they did, you would certainly never get back to England."

It was impossible not to laugh. Lady Johnstone did not look at all the sort of person to say witty things, though she was the very incarnation of good humour — except when she thought that Brook was in danger of being married. And every one laughed, Sir Adam first, then Brook, and then the Bowrings. The effect was good. Lady Johnstone was really afflicted with curiosity, and her first questions to Mrs.

Bowring had been asked purely out of a wish to make advances. She was strongly attracted by the quiet, pale face, with its excessive refinement and delicately traced lines of suffering. She felt that the woman had taken life too hard, and it was her instinct to comfort her, and warm her and take care of her, from the first. Brook understood and rejoiced, for he knew his mother's tenacity about her first impressions, and he wished to have her on his side.

After that the ice was broken and the conversation did not flag. Sir Adam looked at Mrs. Bowring from time to time with an expression of uncertainty which sat strangely on his determined features, and whenever any new subject was broached he watched her uneasily until she had spoken. But Mrs. Bowring rarely returned his glances, and her eyes never lingered on his face even when she was speaking to him. Clare, for her part, joined in the conversation, and wondered and waited. Her theory was strengthened by what she saw. Clearly Sir Adam felt uncomfortable in her mother's presence; therefore he had injured her in some way, and doubted whether she had ever forgiven him. But to the girl's quick instinct it was clear that he did not stand to Mrs. Bowring only in the position of one who had harmed her. In some way of love or friendship, he had once been very fond of her.

The youngest woman cannot easily mistake the signs of such bygone intercourse.

When they rose, Mrs. Bowring walked slowly, on her side of the table, so as not to reach the door before Lady Johnstone, who could not move fast under any circumstances. They all went out together upon the terrace.

"Brook," said the fat lady, "I must sit down, or I shall die. You know, my dear—get me one that won't break!"

She laughed a little, as Brook went off to find a solid chair. A few minutes later she was enthroned in safety, her husband on one side of her and Mrs. Bowring on the other, all facing the sea.

"It's too perfect for words!" she exclaimed, in solid and peaceful satisfaction. "Adam, isn't it a dream? You thin people don't know how nice it is to come to anchor in a pleasant place after a long voyage!"

She sighed happily and moved her arms so that their weight was quite at rest without an effort.

Clare and Johnstone walked slowly up and down, passing and repassing, and trying to talk as though neither were aware that there was something unusual in the situation, to say the least of it. At last they stopped at the end farthest away from the others.

Clare and Johnstone walked slowly up and down. — *Page* 202.

"I had no idea that my father had known your mother long ago," said Brook suddenly. "Had you?"

"Yes — of late," answered Clare. "You see my mother wasn't sure, until you told me his first name," she hastened to add.

"Oh — I see. Of course. Stupid of me not to try and bring it into the conversation sooner, wasn't it? But it seems to have been ever so long ago. Don't you think so?"

"Yes. Ever so long ago."

"When they were quite young, I suppose. Your mother must have been perfectly beautiful when she was young. I dare say my father was madly in love with her. It wouldn't be at all surprising, you know, would it? He was a tremendous fellow for falling in love."

"Oh! Was he?" Clare spoke rather coldly.

"You're not angry, are you, because I suggested it?" asked Brook quickly. "I don't see that there's any harm in it. There's no reason why a young man as he was shouldn't have been desperately in love with a beautiful young girl, is there?"

"None whatever," answered Clare. "I was only thinking — it's rather an odd coincidence — do you mind telling me something?"

"Of course not! What is it?"

"Had your father ever a brother — who died?"

"No. He had a lot of sisters — some of them are alive still. Awful old things, my aunts are, too. No, he never had any brother. Why do you ask?"

"Nothing — it's a mere coincidence. Did I ever tell you that my mother was married twice? My father was her second husband. The first had your name."

"Johnstone, with an E on the end of it?"

"Yes — with an E."

"Gad! that's funny!" exclaimed Brook. "Some connection, I dare say. Then we are connected too, you and I, not much though, when one thinks of it. Step-cousin by marriage, and ever so many degrees removed, too."

"You can't call that a connection," said Clare with a little laugh, but her face was thoughtful. "Still, it is odd that she should have known your father well, and should have married a man of the same name — with the E — isn't it?"

"He may have been an own cousin, for all I know," said Brook. "I'll ask. He's sure to remember. He never forgets anything. And it's another coincidence too, that my father should have been married twice, just like your mother, and that I should be the son of the second marriage, too. What odd things happen, when one comes to compare notes!"

While they had walked up and down, Lady Johnstone had paid no attention to them, but she had grown restless as soon as she had seen that they stood still at a distance to talk, and her bright blue eyes turned towards them again and again, with sudden motherly anxiety. At last she could bear it no longer.

"Brook!" she cried. "Brook, my dear boy!" Brook and Clare walked back towards the little group.

"Brook, dear," said Lady Johnstone. "Please come and tell me the names of all the mountains and places we see from here. You know, I always want to know everything as soon as I arrive."

Sir Adam rose from his chair.

"Should you like to take a turn?" he asked, speaking to Mrs. Bowring and standing before her.

She rose in silence and stepped forward, with a quiet, set face, as though she knew that the supreme moment had come.

"Take our chairs," said Sir Adam to Clare and Brook. "We are going to walk about a little."

Mrs. Bowring turned in the direction whence the young people had come, towards the end of the terrace. Sir Adam walked erect beside her.

"Is there a way out at that end?" he asked

in a low voice, when they had gone a little distance.

"No."

"We can't stand there and talk. Where can we go? Isn't there a quiet place somewhere?"

"Do you want to talk to me?" asked Mrs. Bowring, looking straight before her.

"Yes, please," answered Sir Adam, almost sharply, but still in a low tone. "I've waited a long time," he added.

Mrs. Bowring said nothing in answer. They reached the end of the walk, and she turned without pausing.

"The point out there is called the Conca," she said, pointing to the rocks far out below. "It curls round like a shell, you know. Conca means a sea-shell, I think. It seems to be a great place for fishing, for there are always little boats about it in fine weather."

"I remember," replied Sir Adam. "I was here thirty years ago. It hasn't changed much. Are there still those little paper-mills in the valley on the way to Ravello? They used to be very primitive."

They kept up their forced conversation as they passed Lady Johnstone and the young people. Then they were silent again, as they went towards the hotel.

"We'll go through the house," said Mrs.

Bowring, speaking low again. "There's a quiet place on the other side — Clare and your son will have to stay with your wife."

"Yes, I thought of that, when I told them to take our chairs."

In silence they traversed the long tiled corridor with set faces, like two people who are going to do something dangerous and disagreeable together. They came out upon the platform before the deep recess of the rocks in which stood the black cross. There was nobody there.

"We shall not be disturbed out here," said Mrs. Bowring, quietly. "The people in the hotel go to their rooms after luncheon. We will sit down there by the cross, if you don't mind — I'm not so strong as I used to be, you know."

They ascended the few steps which led up to the bench where Clare had sat on that evening which she could not forget, and they sat down side by side, not looking at each other's faces.

A long silence followed. Once or twice Sir Adam shifted his feet uneasily, and opened his mouth as though he were going to say something, but suddenly changed his mind. Mrs. Bowring was the first to speak.

"Please understand," she said slowly, glancing at him sideways, "I don't want you to say anything, and I don't know what you can have

to say. As for my being here, it's very simple.
If I had known that Brook Johnstone was your
son before he had made our acquaintance, and
that you were coming here, I should have gone
away at once. As soon as I knew him I suspected who he was. You must know that he is
like you as you used to be — except your eyes.
Then I said to myself that he would tell you
that he had met us, and that you would of course
think that I had been afraid to meet you. I'm
not. So I stayed. I don't know whether I did
right or wrong. To me it seemed right, and
I'm willing to abide the consequences, if there
are to be any."

"What consequences can there be?" asked
the grey-bearded man, turning his eyes slowly
to her face.

"That depends upon how you act. It might
have been better to behave as though we had
never met, and to let your son introduce you to
me as he introduced you to Clare. We might
have started upon a more formal footing, then.
You have chosen to say that we are old friends.
It's an odd expression to use — but let it stand.
I won't quarrel with it. It does well enough.
As for the position, it's not pleasant for me, but
it must be worse for you. There's not much to
choose. But I don't want you to think that I
expect you to talk about old times unless you

like. If you have anything which you wish to say, I'll hear it all without interrupting you. But I do wish you to believe that I won't do anything nor say anything which could touch your wife. She seems to be happy with you. I hope she always has been and always will be. She knew what she was doing when she married you. God knows, there was publicity enough. Was it my fault? I suppose you've always thought so. Very well, then — say that it was my fault. But don't tell your wife who I am unless she forces you to it out of curiosity."

"Do you think I should wish to?" asked Sir Adam, bitterly.

"No — of course not. But she may ask you who I was and when we met, and all about it. Try and keep her off the subject. We don't want to tell lies, you know."

"I shall say that you were Lucy Waring. That's true enough. You were christened Lucy Waring. She need never know what your last name was. That isn't a lie, is it?"

"Not exactly — under the circumstances."

"And your daughter knows nothing, of course? I want to know how we stand, you see."

"No — only that we have met before. I don't know what she may suspect. And your son?"

"Oh, I suppose he knows. Somebody must have told him."

P

"He doesn't know who I am, though," said Mrs. Bowring, with conviction. "He seems to be more like his mother than like you. He couldn't conceal anything long."

"I wasn't particularly good at that either, as it turned out," said Sir Adam, gravely.

"No, thank God!"

"Do you think it's something to be thankful for? I don't. Things might have gone better afterwards —"

"Afterwards!" The suffering of the woman's life was in the tone and in her eyes.

"Yes, afterwards. I'm an old man, Lucy, and I've seen a great many things since you and I parted, and a great many people. I was bad enough, but I've seen worse men since, who have had another chance and have turned out well."

"Their wives did not love them. I am almost old, too. I loved you, Adam. It was a bad hurt you gave me, and the wound never healed. I married — I had to marry. He was an honest gentleman. Then he was killed. That hurt too, for I was very fond of him — but it did not hurt as the other did. Nothing could."

Her voice shook, and she turned away her face. At least, he should not see that her lip trembled.

"I didn't think you cared," said Sir Adam, and his own voice was not very steady.

She turned upon him almost fiercely, and there was a blue light in her faded eyes.

"I! You thought I didn't care? You've no right to say that — it's wicked of you, and it's cruel. Did you think I married you for your money, Adam? And if I had — should I have given it up to be divorced because you gave jewels to an actress? I loved you, and I wanted your love, or nothing. You couldn't be faithful — commonly, decently faithful, for one year — and I got myself free from you, because I would not be your wife, nor eat your bread, nor touch your hand, if you couldn't love me. Don't say that you ever loved me, except my face. We hadn't been divorced a year when you married again. Don't say that you loved me! You loved your wife — your second wife — perhaps. I hope so. I hope you love her now — and I dare say you do, for she looks happy — but don't say that you ever loved me — just long enough to marry me and betray me!"

"You're hard, Lucy. You're as hard as ever you were twenty years ago," said Adam Johnstone.

As he leaned forward, resting an elbow on his knee, he passed his brown hand across his eyes, and then stared vaguely at the white walls of the old hotel beyond the platform.

"But you know that I'm right," answered

Mrs. Bowring. "·Perhaps I'm hard, too. I'm sorry. You said that you had been mad, I remember — I don't like to think of all you said, but you said that. And I remember thinking that I had been much more mad than you, to have married you, but that I should soon be really mad — raving mad — if I remained your wife. I couldn't. I should have died. Afterwards I thought it would have been better if I had died then. But I lived through it. Then, after the death of my old aunt, I was alone. What was I to do? I was poor and lonely, and a divorced woman, though the right had been on my side. Richard Bowring knew all about it, and I married him. I did not love you any more, then, but I told him the truth when I told him that I could never love any one again. He was satisfied — so we were married."

" I don't blame you," said Sir Adam.

" Blame me! No — it would hardly be for you to blame me, if I could make anything of the shreds of my life which I had saved from yours. For that matter — you were free too. It was soon done, but why should I blame you for that? You were free — by the law — to go where you pleased, to love again, and to marry at once. You did. Oh no! I don't blame you for that!"

Both were silent for some time. But Mrs.

Bowring's eyes still had an indignant light in them, and her fingers twitched nervously from time to time. Sir Adam stared stolidly at the white wall, without looking at his former wife.

"I've been talking about myself," she said at last. "I didn't mean to, for I need no justification. When you said that you wanted to say something, I brought you here so that we could be alone. What was it? I should have let you speak first."

"It was this." He paused, as though choosing his words. "Well, I don't know," he continued presently. "You've been saying a good many things about me that I would have said myself. I've not denied them, have I? Well, it's this. I wanted to see you for years, and now we've met. We may not meet again, Lucy, though I dare say we may live a long time. I wish we could, though. But of course you don't care to see me. I was your husband once, and I behaved like a brute to you. You wouldn't want me for a friend now that I am old."

He waited, but she said nothing.

"Of course you wouldn't," he continued. "I shouldn't, in your place. Oh, I know! If I were dying or starving, or very unhappy, you would be capable of doing anything for me, out of sheer goodness. You're only just to people who aren't suffering. You were always like that in the old days. It's so much the worse for us. I have nothing about me to excite your pity. I'm strong, I'm well, I'm very rich, I'm relatively happy. I don't know how much I cared for my wife when I married her, but she has been a good wife, and I'm very fond of her now, in my own way. It wasn't a good action, I admit, to marry her at all. She was the beauty of her year and the best match of the season, and I was just divorced, and every one's hand was against me. I thought I would show them what I could do, winged as I was, and I got her. No; it wasn't a thing to be proud of. But somehow we hit it off, and she stuck to me, and I grew fond of her because she did, and here we are as you see us, and Brook is a fine fellow, and likes me. I like him too. He's honest and faithful, like his mother. There's no justice and no logic in this world, Lucy. I was a good-for-nothing in the old days. Circumstances have made me decently good, and a pretty happy man besides, as men go. I couldn't ask for any pity if I tried."

"No; you're not to be pitied. I'm glad you're happy. I don't wish you any harm."

"You might, and I shouldn't blame you. But all that isn't what I wished to say. I'm getting old, and we may not meet any more after this. If you wish me to go away, I'll go. We'll leave the place tomorrow."

"No. Why should you? It's a strange situation, as we were to-day at table. You with your wife beside, and your divorced wife opposite you, and only you and I knowing it. I suppose you think, somehow — I don't know — that I might be jealous of your wife. But twenty-seven years make a difference, Adam. It's half a lifetime. It's so utterly past that I sha'n't realise it. If you like to stay, then stay. No harm can come of it, and that was so very long ago. Is that what you want to say?"

"No." He hesitated. "I want you to say that you forgive me," he said, in a quick, hoarse voice.

His keen dark eyes turned quickly to her face, and he saw how very pale she was, and how the shadows had deepened under her eyes, and her fingers twitched nervously as they clasped one another in her lap.

"I suppose you think I'm sentimental," he said, looking at her. "Perhaps I am; but it would mean a good deal to me if you would just say it."

There was something pathetic in the appeal, and something young too, in spite of his grey beard and furrowed face. Still Mrs. Bowring said nothing. It meant almost too much to her, even after twenty-seven years. This old man had taken her, an innocent young girl, had married her, had betrayed her while she dearly loved him, and had blasted her life at the beginning. Even now it was hard to forgive. The suffering was not old, and the sight of his face had touched the quick again. Barely ten minutes had passed since the pain had almost wrung the tears from her.

"You can't," said the old man, suddenly. "I see it. It's too much to ask, I suppose, and I've never done anything to deserve it."

The pale face grew paler, but the hands were still, and grasped each other, firm and cold. The lips moved, but no sound came. Then a moment, and they moved again.

"You're mistaken, Adam. I do forgive you."

He caught the two hands in his, and his face shivered.

"God bless you, dear," he tried to say, and he kissed the hands twice.

When Mrs. Bowring looked up he was sitting beside her, just as before ; but his face was terribly drawn, and strange, and a great tear had trickled down the furrowed brown cheek into the grey beard.

"God bless you, dear," he tried to say, and he kissed the hands
twice. — *Page* 216.

CHAPTER XI

LADY JOHNSTONE was one of those perfectly frank and honest persons who take no trouble to conceal their anxieties. From the fact that when she had met him on the way up to the hotel Brook had been walking alone with Clare Bowring, she had at once argued that a considerable intimacy existed between the two. Her meeting with Clare's mother, and her sudden fancy for the elder woman, had momentarily allayed her fears, but they revived when it became clear to her that Brook sought every possible opportunity of being alone with the young girl. She was an eminently practical woman, as has been said, which perhaps accounted for her having made a good husband out of such a man as Adam Johnstone had been in his youth. She had never seen Brook devote himself to a young girl before now. She saw that Clare was good to look at, and she promptly concluded that Brook must be in love. The conclusion was perfectly correct, and Lady Johnstone soon grew very nervous. Brook was too young to marry, and even if he had been old enough his mother thought that he might have made a better choice. At all events he should not entangle himself in an engagement with the girl ; and she began systematically to interfere with his attempts to be alone with her   Brook was as frank as herself. He charged her with trying to keep him from Clare, and she did not deny that he was right. This led to a discussion on the third day after the Johnstones' arrival.

" You mustn't make a fool of yourself, Brook, dear," said Lady Johnstone. " You are not old enough to marry. Oh, I know, you are five-and-twenty, and ought to have come to years of discretion. But you haven't, dear boy. Don't forget that you are Adam Johnstone's son, and that you may be expected to do all the things that he did before I married him. And he did a good many things, you know. I'm devoted to your father, and if he were in the room I should tell you just what I am telling you now. Before I married him he had about a thousand flirtations, and he had been married too, and had gone off with an actress — a shocking affair altogether ! And his wife had divorced him. She must have been one of those horrible women who can't forgive, you know. Now, my dear boy, you aren't a bit better than your father, and that pretty Clare Bowring looks as though she would never forgive anybody who did anything she didn't like. Have you asked her to marry you?"

" Good heavens, no ! " cried Brook. " She wouldn't look at me ! "

" Wouldn't look at you ? That's simply ridiculous, you know! She'd marry you out of hand — unless she's perfectly idiotic. And she doesn't look that. Leave. her alone, Brook. Talk to the mother. She's one of the most delightful women I ever met. She has a dear, quiet way with her — like a very thoroughbred white cat that's been ill and wants to be petted."

" What extraordinary ideas you have, mother ! " laughed Brook. " But on general principles I don't see why I shouldn't marry Miss Bowring, if she'll have me. Why not ? Her father was a gentleman, you like her mother, and as for herself — "

" Oh, I've nothing against her. It's all against you, Brook dear. You are such a dreadful flirt, you know ! You'll get tired of the poor girl and make her miserable. I'm sure she isn't practical, as I am. The very first time you look at some one else she'll get on a tragic horse and charge the crockery — and there will be a most awful smash ! It's not easy to manage you Johnstones when you think you are in love. I ought to know ! "

"I say, mother," said Brook, "has anybody been telling you stories about me lately?"

"Lately? Let me see. The last I heard was that Mrs. Crosby — the one you all call Lady Fan — was going to get a divorce so as to marry you."

"Oh — you heard that, did you?"

"Yes — everybody was talking about it and asking me whether it was true. It seems that she was with that party that brought you here. She left them at Naples, and came home at once by land, and they said she was giving out that she meant to marry you. I laughed, of course. But people wouldn't talk about you so much, dear boy, if there were not so much to talk about. I know that you would never do anything so idiotic as that, and if Mrs. Crosby chooses to flirt with you, that's her affair. She's older than you, and knows more about it. But this is quite another thing. This is serious. You sha'n't make love to that nice girl, Brook. You sha'n't! I'll do something dreadful, if you do. I'll tell her all about Mrs. Leo Cairngorm or somebody like that. But you sha'n't marry her and ruin her life."

"You're going in for philanthropy, mother," said Brook, growing red. "It's something new. You never made a fuss before."

"No, of course not. You never were so fool-

"I'll tell the mother, too. I'll frighten them all, till they can't bear the sight of you." — *Page* 221.

ish before, my dear boy. I'm not bad myself,
I believe. But you are, every one of you, and
I love you all, and the only way to do anything
with you is to let you run wild a little first. It's
the only practical, sensible way. And you've
only just begun — how in the world do you dare
to think of marrying? Upon my word, it's too
bad. I won't wait. I'll frighten the girl to
death with stories about you, until she refuses
to speak to you! But I've taken a fancy to her
mother, and you sha'n't make the child miserable. You sha'n't, Brook. Oh, I've made up
my mind! You sha'n't. I'll tell the mother
too. I'll frighten them all, till they can't bear
the sight of you."

Lady Johnstone was energetic, as well as
original, in spite of her abnormal size, and
Brook knew that she was quite capable of carrying out her threat, and more also.

"I may be like my father in some ways," he
answered. "But I'm a good deal like you too,
mother. I'm rather apt to stick to what I like,
you know. Besides, I don't believe you would
do anything of the kind. And she isn't inclined
to like me, as it is. I believe she must have
heard some story or other. Don't make things
any worse than they are."

"Then don't lose your head and ask her to
marry you after a fortnight's acquaintance,

Brook, because she'll accept you, and you will make her perfectly wretched."

He saw that it was not always possible to argue with his mother, and he said nothing more. But he reflected upon her point of view, and he saw that it was not altogether unjust, as she knew him. She could not possibly understand that what he felt for Clare Bowring bore not the slightest resemblance to what he had felt for Lady Fan, if, indeed, he had felt anything at all, which he considered doubtful now that it was over, though he would have been angry enough at the suggestion a month earlier. To tell the truth, he felt quite sure of himself at the present time, though all his sensations were more or less new to him. And his mother's sudden and rather eccentric opposition unexpectedly strengthened his determination. He might laugh at what he called her originality, but he could not afford to jest at the prospect of her giving Clare an account of his life. She was quite capable of it, and would probably do it.

These preoccupations, however, were as nothing compared with the main point — the certainty that Clare would refuse him, if he offered himself to her, and when he left his mother he was in a very undetermined state of mind. If he should ask Clare to marry him now, she

would refuse him. But if his mother inter-
fered, it would be much worse a week hence.

At last, as ill-luck would have it, he came
upon her unexpectedly in the corridor, as he
came out, and they almost ran against each
other.

"Won't you come out for a bit?" he asked
quickly and in a low voice.

"Thanks — I have some letters to write,"
answered the young girl. "Besides, it's much
too hot. There isn't a breath of air."

"Oh, it's not really hot, you know," said
Brook, persuasively.

"Then it's making a very good pretence!"
laughed Clare.

"It's ever so much cooler out of doors. If
you'll only come out for one minute, you'll see.
Really — I'm in earnest."

"But why should I go out if I don't want to?"
asked the young girl.

"Because I asked you to —"

"Oh, that isn't a reason, you know," she
laughed again.

"Well, then, because you really would, if I
hadn't asked you, and you only refuse out of a
spirit of opposition," suggested Brook.

"Oh — do you think so? Do you think I
generally do just the contrary of what I'm asked
to do?"

"Of course, everybody knows that, who knows you." Brook seemed amused at the idea.

"If you think that — well, I'll come, just for a minute, if it's only to show you that you are quite wrong."

"Thanks, awfully. Sha'n't we go for the little walk that was interrupted when my people came the other day?"

"No — it's too hot, really. I'll walk as far as the end of the terrace and back — once. Do you mind telling me why you are so tremendously anxious to have me come out this very minute?"

"I'll tell you — at least, I don't know that I can — wait till we are outside. I should like to be out with you all the time, you know — and I thought you might come, so I asked you."

"You seem rather confused," said Clare gravely.

"Well, you know," Brook answered as they walked along towards the dazzling green light that filled the door, "to tell the truth, between one thing and another — " He did not complete the sentence.

"Yes?" said Clare, sweetly. "Between one thing and another — what were you going to say?"

Brook did not answer as they went out into the hot, blossom-scented air, under the spreading vines.

"Do you mean to say it's cooler here than indoors?" asked the young girl in a tone of resignation.

"Oh, it's much cooler! There's a breeze at the end of the walk."

"The sea is like oil," observed Clare. "There isn't the least breath."

"Well," said Brook, "it can't be really hot, because it's only the first week in June after all."

"This isn't Scotland. It's positively boiling, and I wish I hadn't come out. Beware of first impulses — they are always right!"

But she glanced sideways at his face, for she knew that something was in the air. She was not sure what to expect of him just then, but she knew that there was something to expect. Her instinct told her that he meant to speak and to say more than he had yet said. It told her that he was going to ask her to marry him, then and there, in the blazing noon, under the vines, but her modesty scouted the thought as savouring of vanity. At all events she would prevent him from doing it if she could.

"Lady Johnstone seems to like this place," she said, with a sudden effort at conversation. "She says that she means to make all sorts of expeditions."

"Of course she will," answered Brook, in a

Q

half-impatient tone. "But, please — I don't want to talk about my mother or the landscape. I really did want to speak to you, because I can't stand this sort of thing any longer, you know."

"What sort of thing?" asked Clare innocently, raising her eyes to his, as they reached the end of the walk.

It was very hot and still. Not a breath stirred the young vine-leaves overhead, and the scent of the last orange-blossoms hung in the motionless air. The heat rose quivering from the sea to southward, and the water lay flat as a mirror under the glory of the first summer's day.

They stood still. Clare felt nervous, and tried to think of something to say which might keep him from speaking, and destroy the effect of her last question. But it was too late now. He was pale, for him, and his eyes were very bright.

"I can't live without you — it comes to that. Can't you see?"

The short plain words shook oddly as they fell from his lips. The two stood quite still, each looking into the other's face. Brook grew paler still, but the colour rose in Clare's cheeks. She tried to meet his eyes steadily, without feeling that he could control her.

"I'm sorry," she said, "I'm very sorry."

"You sha'n't say that," he answered, cutting

her words with his, and sharply.   " I'm tired of
hearing it.   I'm glad I love you, whatever you
do to me; and you must get to like me.   You
must.   I tell you I can't live without you."

" But if I can't —" Clare tried to say.

" You can — you must — you shall ! " broke
in Brook, hoarsely, his eyes growing brighter
and fiercer.   " I didn't know what it was to
love anybody, and now that I know, I can't
live without it, and I won't."

" But if — "

" There is no ' if,' " he cried, in his low strong
voice, fixing her eyes with his.   " There's no
question of my going mad, or dying, or anything
half so weak, because I won't take no.   Oh, you
may say it a hundred times, but it won't help
you.   I tell you I love you.   Do you understand
what that means ?   I'm in God's own earnest.
I'll give you my life, but I won't give you up.
I'll take you somehow, whether you will or not,
and I'll hide you somewhere, but you sha'n't
get away from me as long as you live."

" You must be mad ! " exclaimed the young
girl, scarcely above her breath, half-frightened,
and unable to loose her eyes from the fascination
of his.

" No, I'm not mad ; only you've never seen
any one in earnest before, and you've been con-
demning me without evidence all along.   But it

must stop now. You must tell me what it is, for I have a right to know. Tell me what it all is. I will know — I will. Look at me; you can't look away till you tell me."

Clare felt his power, and felt that his eyes were dazzling her, and that if she did not escape from them she must yield and tell him. She tried, and her eyelids quivered. Then she raised her hand to cover her own eyes, in a desperate attempt to keep her secret. He caught it and held it, and still looked. She turned pale suddenly. Then her words came mechanically.

"I was out there when you said 'good-bye' to Lady Fan. I heard everything, from first to last."

He started in surprise, and the colour rose suddenly to his face. He did not look away yet, but Clare saw the blush of shame in his face, and felt that his power diminished, while hers grew all at once, to overmaster him in turn.

"It's scarcely a fortnight since you betrayed her," she said, slowly and distinctly, "and you expect me to like you and to believe that you are in earnest."

His shame turned quickly to anger.

"So you listened!" he exclaimed.

"Yes, I listened," she answered, and her words came easily, then, in self-defence — for she had thought of it all very often. "I didn't know

who you were. My mother and I had been sitting beside the cross in the shadow of the cave,
and she went in to finish a letter, leaving me
there. Then you two came out talking. Before
I knew what was happening you had said too
much. I felt that if I had been in Lady Fan's
place I would far rather never know that a
stranger was listening. So I sat still, and I
could not help hearing. How was I to know
that you meant to stay here until I heard you
say so to her? And I heard everything. You
are ashamed now that you know that I know.
Do you wonder that I disliked you from the
first?"

"I don't see why you should," answered Brook
stubbornly. "If you do — you do. That doesn't
change matters —"

"You betrayed her!" cried Clare indignantly. "You forgot that I heard all you said
— how you promised to marry her if she could
get a divorce. It was horrible, and I never
dreamt of such things, but I heard it. And then
you were tired of her, I suppose, and you changed
your mind, and calmly told her that it was all
a mistake. Do you expect any woman, who
has seen another treated in that way, to forget?
Oh, I saw her face, and I heard her sob. You
broke her heart for your amusement. And it
was only a fortnight ago!"

She had the upper hand now, and she turned from him with a last scornful glance, and looked over the low wall at the sea, wondering how he could have held her with his eyes a moment earlier. Brook stood motionless beside her, and there was silence. He might have found much in self-defence, but there was not one word of it which he could tell her. Perhaps she might find out some day what sort of person Lady Fan was, but his own lips were closed. That was his view of what honour meant.

Clare felt that her breath came quickly, and that the colour was deep in her cheeks as she gazed at the flat, hot sea. For a moment she felt a woman's enormous satisfaction in being absolutely unanswerable. Then, all at once, she had a strong sensation of sickness, and a quick pain shot sharply through her just below the heart. She steadied herself by the wall with her hands, and shut her lips tightly.

She had refused him as well as accused him. He would go away in a few moments, and never try to be alone with her again. Perhaps he would leave Amalfi that very day. It was impossible that she should really care for him, and yet, if she did not care, she would not ask the next question. Then he spoke to her. His voice was changed and very quiet now.

"I'm sorry you heard all that," he said. "I

don't wonder that you've got a bad opinion of me, and I suppose I can't say anything just now to make you change it. You heard, and you think you have a right to judge. Perhaps I shouldn't even say this — you heard me then, and you have heard me now. There's a difference, you'll admit. But all that you heard then, and all that you have told me now, can't change the truth, and you can't make me love you less, whatever you do. I don't believe I'm that sort of man."

" I should have thought you were," said Clare bitterly, and regretting the words as soon as they were spoken.

" It's natural that you should think so. At the same time, it doesn't follow that because a man doesn't love one woman he can't possibly love another."

" That's simply brutal!" exclaimed the young girl, angry with him unreasonably because the argument was good.

" It's true, at all events. I didn't love Mrs. Crosby, and I told her so. You may think me a brute if you like, but you heard me say it, if you heard anything, so I suppose I may quote myself. I do love you, and I have told you so — the fact that I can't say it in choice language doesn't make it a lie. I'm not a man in a book, and I'm in earnest."

"Please stop," said Clare, as she heard the hoarse strength coming back in his voice.

"Yes — I know. I've said it before, and you don't care to hear it again. You can't kill it by making me hold my tongue, you know. It only makes it worse. You'll see that I'm in earnest in time — then you'll change your mind. But I can't change mine. I can't live without you, whatever you may think of me now."

It was a strange wooing, very unlike anything she had ever dreamt of, if she had allowed herself to dream of such things. She asked herself whether this could be the same man who had calmly and cynically told Lady Fan that he did not love her and could not think of marrying her. He had been cool and quiet enough then. That gave strength to the argument he used now. She had seen him with another woman, and now she saw him with herself and heard him. She was surprised and almost taken from her feet by his rough vehemence. He surely did not speak as a man choosing his words, certainly not as one trying to produce an effect. But then, on that evening at the Acropolis — the thought of that scene pursued her — he had doubtless spoken just as roughly and vehemently to Lady Fan, and had seemed just as much in earnest. And suddenly Lady Fan was hateful to her, and she almost

ceased to pity her at all. But for Lady Fan —
well, it might have been different. She should
not have blamed herself for liking him, for loving him perhaps, and his words would have had
another ring.

He still stood beside her, watching her, and
she was afraid to turn to him lest he should see
something in her face which she meant to hide.
But she could speak quietly enough, resting her
hands on the wall and looking out to sea. It
would be best to be a little formal, she thought.
The sound of his own name spoken distinctly
and coldly would perhaps warn him not to go
too far.

"Mr. Johnstone," she said, steadying her
voice, "this can't go on. I never meant to tell
you what I knew, but you have forced me to it.
I don't love you — I don't like a man who can
do such things, and I never could. And I can't
let you talk to me in this way any more. If we
must meet, you must behave just as usual. If
you can't, I shall persuade my mother to go
away at once."

"I shall follow you," said Brook. "I told
you so the other day. You can't possibly go to
any place where I can't go too."

"Do you mean to persecute me, Mr. Johnstone?" she asked.

"I love you."

"I hate you!"

"Yes, but you won't always. Even if you do, I shall always love you just as much."

Her eyes fell before his.

"Do you mean to say that you can really love a woman who hates you?" she asked, looking at one of her hands as it rested on the wall.

"Of course. Why not? What has that to do with it?"

The question was asked so simply and with such honest surprise that Clare looked up again. He was smiling a little sadly.

"But — I don't understand — " she hesitated.

"Do you think it's like a bargain?" he asked quietly. "Do you think it's a matter of exchange — 'I will love you if you'll love me'? Oh no! It's not that. I can't help it. I'm not my own master. I've got to love you, whether I like it or not. But since I do — well, I've said the rest, and I won't repeat it. I've told you that I'm in earnest, and you haven't believed me. I've told you that I love you, and you won't even believe that —"

"No — I can believe that, well enough, now. You do to-day, perhaps. At least you think you do."

"Well — you don't believe it, then. What's the use of repeating it? If I could talk well, it would be different, but I'm not much of a talker, at best, and just now I can't put two words together. But I — I mean lots of things that I can't say, and perhaps wouldn't say, you know. At least, not just now."

He turned from her and began to walk up and down across the narrow terrace, towards her and away from her, his hands in his pockets, and his head a little bent. She watched him in silence for some time. Perhaps if she had hated him as much as she said that she did, she would have left him then and gone into the house. Something, good or evil, tempted her to speak.

" What do you mean, that you wouldn't say now? " she asked.

" I don't know," he answered gruffly, still walking up and down, ten steps each way. " Don't ask me — I told you one thing. I shall follow you wherever you go."

" And then? " asked Clare, still prompted by some genius, good or bad.

" And then? " Brook stopped and stared at her rather wildly. " And then? If I can't get you in any other way — well, I'll take you, that's all! It's not a very pretty thing to say, is it? "

" It doesn't sound a very probable thing to do, either," answered Clare. " I'm afraid you are out of your mind, Mr. Johnstone."

" You've driven most things out of it since I loved you," answered Brook, beginning to walk again. "You've made me say things that I shouldn't have dreamed of saying to any woman, much less to you. And you've made me think of doing things that looked perfectly mad a week ago." He stopped before her. "Can't you see? Can't you understand? Can't you feel how I love you?"

"Don't — please don't!" she said, beginning to be frightened at his manner again.

"Don't what? Don't love you? Don't live, then — don't exist — don't anything! What would it all matter, if I didn't love you? Meanwhile, I do, and by the — no! What's the use of talking? You might laugh. You'd make a fool of me, if you hadn't killed the fool out of me with too much earnest — and what's left can't talk, though it can do something better worth while than a lot of talking."

Clare began to think that the heat had hurt his head. And all the time, in a secret, shamefaced way, she was listening to his incoherent sentences and rough exclamations, and remembering them one by one, and every one. And she looked at his pale face, and saw the queer light in his blue eyes, and the squaring of his jaw — and then and long afterwards the whole picture, with its memory of words, hot, broken, and confused, meant earnest love in her thoughts. No man in his senses, wishing to play a part and

"Please don't!" she said, beginning to be frightened at his manner again. — *Page* 236.

produce an impression upon a woman, would have acted as he did, and she knew it. It was the rough, real thing — the raw strength of an honest man's uncontrolled passion that she saw — and it told her more of love in a few minutes than all she had heard or read in her whole life. But while it was before her, alive and throbbing and incoherent of speech, it frightened her.

"Come," she said nervously, "we mustn't stay out here any longer, talking in this way."

He stopped again, close before her, and his eyes looked dangerous for an instant. Then he straightened himself, and seemed to swallow something with an effort.

"All right," he answered. "I don't want to keep you out here in the heat."

He faced about, and they walked slowly towards the house. When they reached the door he stood aside. She saw that he did not mean to go in, and she paused an instant on the threshold, looked at him gravely, and nodded before she entered. Again he bent his head, and said nothing. She left him standing there, and went straight to her room.

Then she sat down before a little table on which she wrote her letters, near the window, and she tried to think. But it was not easy, and everything was terribly confused. She rested her elbows upon the small desk and pressed her fingers to her eyes, as though to drive away the sight that would come back. Then she dropped her hands suddenly and opened her eyes wide, and stared at the wall-paper before her. And it came back very vividly between her and the white plaster, and she heard his voice again — but she was smiling now.

She started violently, for she felt two hands laid unexpectedly upon her shoulders, and some one kissed her hair. She had not heard her mother's footstep, nor the opening and shutting of the door, nor anything but Brook Johnstone's voice.

"What is it, my darling?" asked the elder woman, bending down over her daughter's shoulder. "Has anything happened?"

Clare hesitated a moment, and then spoke, for the habit of her confidence was strong. "He has asked me to marry him, mother —"

In her turn Mrs. Bowring started, and then rested one hand on the table.

"You? You?" she repeated, in a low and troubled voice. "You marry Adam Johnstone's son?"

"No, mother — never," answered the young girl.

"Thank God!"

And Mrs. Bowring sank into a chair, shivering as though she were cold.

CHAPTER XII

BROOK felt in his pocket mechanically for his pipe, as a man who smokes generally takes to something of the sort at great moments in his life, from sheer habit. He went through the operation of filling and lighting with great precision, almost unconscious of what he was doing, and presently he found himself smoking and sitting on the wall just where Clare had leaned against it during their interview. In three minutes his pipe had gone out, but he was not aware of the fact, and sat quite still in his place, staring into the shrubbery which grew at the back of the terrace.

He was conscious that he had talked and acted wildly, and quite unlike the self with which he had been long acquainted; and the consciousness was anything but pleasant. He wondered where Clare was, and what she might be thinking of him at that moment. But as he thought of her his former mood returned, and he felt that he was not ashamed of what he had done and said. Then he realised, all at once, for the second time, that Clare had been on the platform on that first night, and he tried to

recall everything that Lady Fan and he had
said to each other.

No such thing had ever happened to him
before, and he had a sensation of shame and
distress and anger, as he went over the scene,
and thought of the innocent young girl who had
sat in the shadow and heard it all. She had
accidentally crossed the broad, clear line of
demarcation which he drew between her kind
and all the tribe of Lady Fans and Mrs. Cairn-
gorms whom he had known. He felt somehow
as though it were his fault, and as though he
were responsible to Clare for what she had heard
and seen. The sensation of shame deepened,
and he swore bitterly under his breath. It was
one of those things which could not be undone,
and for which there was no reparation possible.
Yet it was like an insult to Clare. For a man
who had lately been rough to the girl, almost to
brutality, he was singularly sensitive perhaps.
But that did not strike him. When he had
told her that he loved her, he had been too much
in earnest to pick and choose his expressions.
But when he had spoken to Lady Fan, he might
have chosen and selected and polished his
phrases so that Clare should have understood
nothing — if he had only known that she had
been sitting up there by the cross in the dark.
And again he cursed himself bitterly.

It was not because her knowing the facts had spoilt everything and given her a bad impression of him from the first: that might be set right in time, even now, and he did not wish her to marry him believing him to be an angel of light. It was that she should have seen something which she should not have seen, for her innocence's sake — something which, in a sense, must have offended and wounded her maidenliness. He would have struck any man who could have laughed at his sensitiveness about that. The worst of it — and he went back to the idea again and again —was that nothing could be done to mend matters, since it was all so completely in the past.

He sat on the wall and pulled at his briar-root pipe, which had gone out and was quite cold by this time, though he hardly knew it. He had plenty to think of, and things were not going straight at all. He had pretended indifference when his mother had told him how Lady Fan meant to get a divorce and how she was telling her intimate friends under the usual vain promises of secrecy that she meant to marry Adam Johnstone's son as soon as she should be free. Brook had told her plainly enough that he would not marry her in any case, but he asked himself whether the world might not say that he should, and whether in that case it might

R

not turn out to be a question of honour. He had
secretly thought of that before now, and in the
sudden depression of spirits which came upon
him as a reaction he cursed himself a third
time for having told Clare Bowring that he
loved her, while such a matter as Lady Fan's
divorce was still hanging over him as a possibility.

Sitting on the wall, he swung his legs angrily,
striking his heels against the stones in his perplexed discontent with the ordering of the uni-
verse. Things looked very black. He wished
that he could see Clare again, and that, somehow, he could talk it all over with her. Then
he almost laughed at the idea. She would tell
him that she disliked him — he was sick of the
sound of the word — and that it was his duty to
marry Lady Fan. What could she know of Lady
Fan ? He could not tell her that the little lady
in the white serge, being rather desperate, had
got herself asked to go with the party for the
express purpose of throwing herself at his head,
as the current phrase gracefully expresses it,
and with the distinct intention of divorcing her
husband in order to marry Brook Johnstone.
He could not tell Clare that he had made love
to Lady Fan to get rid of her, as another common expression put it, with a delicacy worthy
of modern society. He could not tell her that

Lady Fan, who was clever but indiscreet, had
unfolded her scheme to her bosom friend Mrs.
Leo Cairngorm, or that Mrs. Cairngorm, unknown to Lady Fan, had been a very devoted
friend of Brook's, and was still fond of him, and
secretly hated Lady Fan, and had therefore unfolded the whole plan to Brook before the party
had started; or that on that afternoon at sunset
on the Acropolis he had not at all assented to
Lady Fan's mad proposal, as she had represented that he had when they had parted on the
platform at Amalfi; he could not tell Clare any
of these things, for he felt that they were not
fit for her to hear.   And if she knew none of
them she must judge him out of her ignorance.
Brook wished that some supernatural being
with a gift for solving hard problems would
suddenly appear and set things straight.

Instead, he saw the man who brought the
letters just entering the hotel, and he rose by
force of habit and went to the office to see if
there were anything for him.

There was one, and it was from Lady Fan,
by no means the first she had written since she
had gone to England.   And there were several
for Sir Adam and two for Lady Johnstone.
Brook took them all, and opened his own at
once.   He did not belong to that class of people
who put off reading disagreeable correspond-

ence. While he read he walked slowly along the corridor.

Lady Fan was actually consulting a firm of solicitors with a view to getting a divorce. She said that she of course understood his conduct on that last night at Amalfi — the whole plan must have seemed unrealisable to him then — she would forgive him. She refused to believe that he would ruin her in cold blood, as she must be ruined if she got a divorce from Crosby, and if Brook would not marry her; and much more.

Why should she be ruined? Brook asked himself. If Crosby divorced her on Brook's account, it would be another matter altogether. But she was going to divorce Crosby, who was undoubtedly a beast, and her reputation would be none the worse for it. People would only wonder why she had not done it before, and so would Crosby, unless he took it into his head to examine the question from a financial point of view. For Crosby was, or had been, rich, and Lady Fan had no money of her own, and Crosby was quite willing to let her spend a good deal, provided she left him in peace. How in the world could Clare ever know all the truth about such people? It would be an insult to her to think that she could understand half of it, and she would not think the better of him unless she could understand it all. The situation did not seem to admit of any solution in that way. All he could hope for was that Clare might change her mind. When she should be older she would understand that she had made a mistake, and that the world was not merely a high-class boarding-school for young ladies, in which all the men were employed as white-chokered professors of social righteousness. That seemed to be her impression, he thought, with a resentment which was not against her in particular, but against all young girls in general, and which did not prevent him from feeling that he would not have had it otherwise for anything in the world.

He stuffed the letter into his pocket, and went in search of his father. He was strongly inclined to lay the whole matter before him, and to ask the old gentleman's advice. He had reason to believe that Sir Adam had been in worse scrapes than this when he had been a young man, and somehow or other nobody had ever thought the worse of him. He was sure to be in his room at that hour, writing letters. Brook knocked and went in. It was about eleven o'clock.

Sir Adam, gaunt and grey, and clad in a cashmere dressing-jacket, was extended upon all the chairs which the little cell-like room contained, close by the open window. He had a very thick cigarette between his lips, and a half-emptied glass of brandy and soda stood on the corner of a table at his elbow. He had not failed to drink one brandy and soda every morning at eleven o'clock for at least a quarter of a century.

His keen old eyes turned sharply to Brook as the latter entered, and a smile lighted up his furrowed face, but instantly disappeared again; for the young man's features betrayed something of what he had gone through during the last hour.

"Anything wrong, boy?" asked Sir Adam quickly. "Have a brandy and soda and a pipe with me. Oh, letters! It's devilish hard that the post should find a man out in this place! Leave them there on the table."

Brook relighted his pipe. His father took one leg from one of the chairs, which he pushed towards his son with his foot by way of an invitation to sit down.

"What's the matter?" he asked, renewing his question. "You've got into another scrape, have you? Mrs. Crosby — of all women in the world. Your mother told me that ridiculous story. Wants to divorce Crosby and marry you, does she? I say, boy, it's time this sort of nonsense stopped, you know. One of these days you'll be caught. There are cleverer women in the world than Mrs. Crosby."

" Oh ! she's not clever," answered Brook thoughtfully.

" Well, what's the foundation of the story? What the dickens did you go with those people for, when you found out that she was coming? You knew the sort of woman she was, I suppose? What happened? You made love to her, of course. That was what she wanted. Then she talked of eternal bliss together, and that sort of rot, didn't she? And you couldn't exactly say that you only went in for bliss by the month, could you? And she said, ' By Jove, as you don't refuse, you shall have it for the rest of your life,' and she said to herself that you were richer than Crosby, and a good deal younger, and better-looking, and better socially, and that if you were going to make a fool of yourself she might as well get the benefit of it as well as any other woman. Then she wrote to a solicitor — and now you are in the devil of a scrape. I fancy that's the history of the case, isn't it?"

" I wish you wouldn't talk about women in that sort of way, Governor!" exclaimed Brook, by way of answer.

" Don't be an ass!" answered Sir Adam. " There are women one can talk about in that way, and women one can't. Mrs. Crosby is one of the first kind. I distinguish between

'women' and 'woman.' Don't you? Woman
means something to most of us — something a
good deal better than we are, which we treat
properly and would cut one another's throats
for. We sinners aren't called upon to respect
women who won't respect themselves. We are
only expected to be civil to them because they
are things in petticoats with complexions.
Don't be an ass, Brook. I don't want to know
what you said to Mrs. Crosby, nor what she
said to you, and you wouldn't be a gentleman
if you told me. That's your affair. But she's
a woman with a consumptive reputation that's
very near giving up the ghost, and that would
have departed this life some time ago if Crosby
didn't happen to be a little worse than she is.
She wants to get a divorce and marry my son
— and that's my affair. Do you remember
the Arab and his slave? 'You've stolen my
money,' said the sheikh. 'That's my business,'
answered the slave. 'And I'm going to beat
you,' said the sheikh. 'That's your business,'
said the slave. It's a similar case, you know,
only it's a good deal worse. I don't want to
know anything that happened before you two
parted. But I've a right to know what Mrs.
Crosby has done since, haven't I? You don't
care to marry her, do you, boy?"

"Marry her! I'd rather cut my throat."

" You needn't do that. Just tell me whether all this is mere talk, or whether she has really been to the solicitor's. If she has, you know, she will get her divorce without opposition. Everybody knows about Crosby."

" It's true," said Brook. " I've just had a letter from her again. I wish I knew what to do ! "

" You can't do anything."

" I can refuse to marry her, can't I ? "

" Oh — you could. But plenty of people would say that you had induced her to get the divorce, and then had changed your mind. She'll count on that, and make the most of it, you may be sure. She won't have a penny when she's divorced, and she'll go about telling everybody that you have ruined her. That won't be pleasant, will it ? "

" No — hardly. I had thought of it."

" You see — you can't do anything without injuring yourself. I can settle the whole affair in half an hour. By return of post you'll get a letter from her telling you that she has abandoned all idea of proceedings against Crosby."

" I'll bet you she doesn't," said Brook.

" Anything you like. It's perfectly simple. I'll just make a will, leaving you nothing at all, if you marry her, and I'll send her a copy to-day. You'll get the answer fast enough."

"By Jove!" exclaimed Brook, in surprise. Then he thoughtfully relighted his pipe and threw the match out of the window. "I say, Governor," he added after a pause, "do you think that's quite — well, quite fair and square, you know?"

"What on earth do you mean?" cried Sir Adam. "Do you mean to tell me that I haven't a perfect right to leave my money as I please? And that the first adventuress who takes a fancy to it has a right to force you into a disgraceful marriage, and that it would be dishonourable of me to prevent it if I could? You're mad, boy! Don't talk such nonsense to me!"

"I suppose I'm an idiot," said Brook. "Things about money so easily get a queer look, you know. It's not like other things, is it?"

"Look here, Brook," answered the old man, taking his feet from the chair on which they rested, and sitting up straight in the low easy chair. "People have said a lot of things about me in my life, and I'll do the world the credit to add that it might have said twice as much with a good show of truth. But nobody ever said that I was mean, nor that I ever disappointed anybody in money matters who had a right to expect something of me. And that's pretty conclusive evidence, because I'm a Scotchman, and we are generally supposed to be a close-fisted tribe. They've said everything about me that the world can say, except that I've told you about my first marriage. She — she got her divorce, you know. She had a perfect right to it."

The old man lit another cigarette, and sipped his brandy and soda thoughtfully.

"I don't like to talk about money," he said in a lower tone. "But I don't want you to think me mean, Brook. I allowed her a thousand a year after she had got rid of me. She never touched it. She isn't that kind. She would rather starve ten times over. But the money has been paid to her account in London for twenty-seven years. Perhaps she doesn't know it. All the better for her daughter, who will find it after her mother's death, and get it all. I only don't want you to think I'm mean, Brook."

"Then she married again — your first wife?" asked the young man, with natural curiosity. "And she's alive still?"

"Yes," answered Sir Adam, thoughtfully. "She married again six years after I did — rather late — and she had one daughter."

"What an odd idea!" exclaimed Brook. "To think that those two people are somewhere about the world. A sort of stray half-sister of

mine, the girl would be — I mean — what would
be the relationship, Governor, since we are talking about it?"

"None whatever," answered the old man, in
a tone so extraordinarily sharp that Brook
looked up in surprise. "Of course not! What
relation could she be? Another mother and
another father — no relation at all."

"Do you mean to say that I could marry
her?" asked Brook idly.

Sir Adam started a little.

"Why — yes — of course you could, as she
wouldn't be related to you."

He suddenly rose, took up his glass, and
gulped down what was left in it. Then he
went and stood before the open window.

"I say, Brook," he began, his back turned to
his son.

"What?" asked Brook, poking his knife into
his pipe to clean it. "Anything wrong?"

"I can't stand this any longer. I've got to
speak to somebody — and I can't speak to your
mother. You won't talk, boy, will you? You
and I have always been good friends."

"Of course! What's the matter with you,
Governor? You can tell me."

"Oh — nothing — that is — Brook, I say,
don't be startled. This Mrs. Bowring is my
divorced wife, you know."

"I say, Brook," he began, his back turned to his son. "What?" asked Brook, poking his knife into his pipe to clean it. "Anything wrong?" — *Page* 252.

" Good God ! "

Sir Adam turned on his heels and met his son's look of horror and astonishment. He had expected an exclamation of surprise, but Brook's voice had fear in it, and he had started from his chair.

" Why do you say ' Good God ' — like that ? " asked the old man. " You're not in love with the girl, are you ? "

" I've just asked her to marry me."

The young man was ghastly pale, as he stood stock-still, staring at his father. Sir Adam was the first to recover something of equanimity, but the furrows in his face had suddenly grown deeper.

" Of course she has accepted you ? " he asked.

" No — she knew about Mrs. Crosby." That seemed sufficient explanation of Clare's refusal. " How awful ! " exclaimed Brook hoarsely, his mind going back to what seemed the main question just then. " How awful for you, Governor ! "

" Well — it's not pleasant," said Sir Adam, turning to the window again. " So the girl refused you," he said, musing, as he looked out. " Just like her mother, I suppose. Brook " — he paused.

" Yes ? "

" So far as I'm concerned, it's not so bad as

you think. You needn't pity me, you know. It's just as well that we should have met — after twenty-seven years."

"She knew you at once, of course?"

"She knew I was your father before I came. And, I say, Brook — she's forgiven me at last."

His voice was low and unsteady, and he resolutely kept his back turned.

"She's one of the best women that ever lived," he said. "Your mother's the other."

There was a long silence, and neither changed his position. Brook watched the back of his father's head.

"You don't mind my saying so to you, Brook?" asked the old man, hitching his shoulders.

"Mind? Why?"

"Oh — well — there's no reason, I suppose. Gad! I wish — I suppose I'm crazy, but I wish to God you could marry the girl, Brook! She's as good as her mother."

Brook said nothing, being very much astonished, as well as disturbed.

"Only — I'll tell you one thing, Brook," said the voice at the window, speaking into space. "If you do marry her — and if you treat her as I treated her mother — " he turned sharply on both heels and waited a minute — "I'll be damned if I don't believe I'd shoot you!"

"I'd spare you the trouble, and do it myself," said Brook, roughly.

They were men, at all events, whatever their faults had been and might be, and they looked at the main things of life in very much the same way, like father like son. Another silence followed Brook's last speech.

"It's settled now, at all events," he said in a decided way, after a long time. "What's the use of talking about it? I don't know whether you mean to stay here. I shall go away this afternoon."

Sir Adam sat down again in his low easy chair, and leaned forward, looking at the pattern of the tiles in the floor, his wrists resting on his knees, and his hands hanging down.

"I don't know," he said slowly. "Let us try and look at it quietly, boy. Don't do anything in a hurry. You're in love with the girl, are you? It isn't a mere flirtation? How the deuce do you know the difference, at your age?"

"Gad!" exclaimed Brook, half angrily. "I know it! that's all. I can't live without her. That is — it's all bosh to talk in that way, you know. One goes on living, I suppose — one doesn't die. You know what I mean. I'd rather lose an arm than lose her — that sort of thing. How am I to explain it to you? I'm in earnest about it. I never asked any girl to marry me

till now. I should think that ought to prove
it. You can't say that I don't know what
married life means."

"Other people's married life," observed Sir
Adam, grimly. "You know something about
that, I'm afraid."

"What difference does it make?" asked Brook.
"I can't marry the daughter of my father's
divorced wife."

"I never heard of a case, simply because such
cases don't arise often. But there's no earthly
reason why you shouldn't. There is no relationship whatever between you. There's no mention of it in the table of kindred and affinity, I
know, simply because it isn't kindred or affinity
in any way. The world may make its observa-
tions. But you may do much more surprising
things than marry the daughter of your father's
divorced wife when you are to have forty thousand pounds a year, Brook. I've found it out in
my time. You'll find it out in yours. And it
isn't as though there were the least thing about
it that wasn't all fair and square and straight
and honourable and legal — and everything
else, including the clergy. I supposed that
the Archbishop of Canterbury wouldn't have
married me the second time, because the Church
isn't supposed to approve of divorces. But I
was married in church all right, by a very good

man. And Church disapproval can't possibly extend to the second generation, you know. Oh no! So far as its being possible goes, there's nothing to prevent your marrying her."

"Except Mrs. Crosby," said Brook. "You'll prove that she doesn't exist either, if you go on. But all that doesn't put things straight. It's a horrible situation, no matter how you look at it. What would my mother say if she knew? You haven't told her about the Bowrings, have you?"

"No," answered Sir Adam, thoughtfully. "I haven't told her anything. Of course she knows the story, but — I'm not sure. Do you think I'm bound to tell her that — who Mrs. Bowring is? Do you think it's anything like not fair to her, just to leave her in ignorance of it? If you think so, I'll tell her at once. That is, I should have to ask Mrs. Bowring first, of course."

"Of course," assented Brook. "You can't do that, unless we go away. Besides, as things are now, what's the use?"

"She'll have to know, if you are engaged to the daughter."

"I'm not engaged to Miss Bowring," said Brook, disconsolately. "She won't look at me. What an infernal mess I've made of my life!"

"Don't be an ass, Brook!" exclaimed Sir Adam, for the third time that morning.

s

"It's all very well to tell me not to be an ass," answered the young man gravely. "I can't mend matters now, and I don't blame her for refusing me. It isn't much more than two weeks since that night. I can't tell her the truth — I wouldn't tell it to you, though I can't prevent your telling it to me, since you've guessed it. She thinks I betrayed Mrs. Crosby, and left her — like the merest cad, you know. What am I to do? I won't say anything against Mrs. Crosby for anything — and if I were low enough to do that I couldn't say it to Miss Bowring. I told her that I'd marry her in spite of herself — carry her off — anything! But of course I couldn't. I lost my head, and talked like a fool."

"She won't think the worse of you for that," observed the old man. "But you can't tell her — the rest. Of course not! I'll see what I can do, Brook. I don't believe it's hopeless at all. I've watched Miss Bowring, ever since we first met you two, coming up the hill. I'll try something —"

"Don't speak to her about Mrs. Crosby, at all events!"

"I don't think I should do anything you wouldn't do yourself, boy," said Sir Adam, with a shade of reproval in his tone. "All I say is that the case isn't so hopeless as you seem to think. Of course you are heavily handicapped, and you are a dog with a bad name, and all the rest of it. The young lady won't change her mind to-day, nor to-morrow either, perhaps. But she wouldn't be a human woman if she never changed it at all."

"You don't know her!" Brook shook his head and began to refill his refractory pipe. "And I don't believe you know her mother either, though you were married to her once. If she is at all what I think she is, she won't let her daughter marry your son. It's not as though anything could happen now to change the situation. It's an old one— it's old, and set, and hard, like a cast. You can't run it into a new mould and make anything else of it. Not even you, Governor — and you are as clever as anybody I know. It's a sheer question of humanity, without any possible outside incident. I've got two things against me which are about as serious as anything can be — the mother's prejudice against you, and the daughter's prejudice against me — both deuced well founded, it seems to me."

"You forget one thing, Brook," said Sir Adam, thoughtfully.

"What's that?"

"Women forgive."

Neither spoke for some time.

"You ought to know," said Brook in a low tone, at last. "They forgive when they love — or have loved. That's the right way to put it, I think."

"Well — put it in that way, if you like. It will just cover the ground. Whatever that young lady may say, she likes you very much. I've seen her watch you, and I'm sure of it."

"How can a woman love a man and hate him at the same time?"

"Why do jealous women sometimes kill their husbands? If they didn't love them they wouldn't care; and if they didn't hate them, they wouldn't kill them. You can't explain it, perhaps, but you can't deny it either. She'll never forgive Mrs. Crosby — perhaps — but she'll forgive you, when she finds out that she can't be happy without you. Stay here quietly, and let me see what I can do."

"You can't do anything, Governor. But I'm grateful to you all the same. And — you know — if there's anything I can do on my side to help you, just now, I'll do it!"

"Thank you, Brook," said the old man, leaning back, and putting up his feet again.

Brook rose and left the room, slowly shutting the door behind him. Then he got his hat and went off for a solitary walk to think matters over. They were grave enough, and all that

He walked slowly and with bent head. — *Page* 261.

his father had said could not persuade him that there was any chance of happiness in his future. There was a sort of horror in the situation, too, and he could not remember ever to have heard of anything like it. He walked slowly, and with bent head.

CHAPTER XIII

SIR ADAM sat still in his place and smoked another thick cigarette before he moved. Then he roused himself, got up, sat down at his table, and took a large sheet of paper from a big leather writing-case.

He had no hesitation about what he meant to put down. In a quarter of an hour he had written out a new will, in which he left his whole fortune to his only son Brook, on condition that Brook did not marry Mrs. Crosby. But if he married her before his father's death he was to have nothing, and if he married her afterwards he was to forfeit the whole, to the uttermost farthing. In either of these cases the property was to go to a third person. Sir Adam hesitated a moment, and then wrote the name of one of his sisters as the conditional legatee. His wife had plenty of money of her own, and besides, the will was a mere formality, drawn up and to be executed solely with a view to checking Lady Fan's enthusiasm. He did not sign it, but folded it smoothly and put it into his pocket. He also took his own pen, for he was particular in matters appertaining to the mechanics of writing, and very neat in all he did.

He went out and wandered up and down the terrace in the heat, but no one was there. Then he knocked at his wife's door, and found her absorbed in an interesting conversation with her maid in regard to matters of dress, as connected with climate. Lady Johnstone at once appealed to him, and the maid eyed him with suspicion, fearing his suggestions. He satisfied her, however, by immediately suggesting that she should go away, whereat she smiled and departed.

Lady Johnstone at once understood that something very serious was in the air. A wonderful good fellowship existed between husband and wife; but they very rarely talked of anything which could not have been discussed, figuratively, on the housetops.

"Brook has got himself into a scrape with that Mrs. Crosby, my dear," said Sir Adam. "What you heard is all more or less true. She has really been to a solicitor, and means to take steps to get a divorce. Of course she could get it easily enough. If she did, people would say that Brook had let her go that far, telling her that he would marry her, and then had changed his mind and left her to her fate. We can't let that happen, you know."

Lady Johnstone looked at her husband with anxiety while he was speaking, and then was silent for a few seconds.

"Oh, you Johnstones! You Johnstones!" she cried at last, shaking her head. "You're perfectly incorrigible!"

"Oh no, my dear," answered Sir Adam; "don't forget me, you know."

"You, Adam!"

Her tone expressed an extraordinary conflict of varying sentiment — amusement, affection, reproach, a retrospective distrust of what might have been, but could not be, considering Sir Adam's age.

"Never mind me, then," he answered. "I've made a will cutting Brook off with nothing if he marries Mrs. Crosby, and I'm going to send her a copy of it to-day. That will be enough, I fancy."

"Adam!"

"Yes — what? Do you disapprove? You always say that you are a practical woman, and you generally show that you are. Why shouldn't I take the practical method of stopping this woman as soon as possible? She wants my money — she doesn't want my son. A fortune with any other name would smell as sweet."

"Yes — but —"

"But what?"

"I don't know — it seems — somehow — "
Lady Johnstone was perplexed to express what
she meant just then. "I mean," she added
suddenly, "it's treating the woman like a mere
adventuress, you know — "

"That's precisely what Mrs. Crosby is, my
dear," answered Sir Adam calmly. "The fact
that she comes of decent people doesn't alter
the case in the least. Nor the fact that she
has one rich husband, and wishes to get another
instead. I say that her husband is rich, but
I'm very sure he has ruined himself in the last
two years, and that she knows it. She is not
the woman to leave him as long as he has
money, for he lets her do anything she pleases,
and pays her well to leave him alone. But he
has got into trouble — and rats leave a sinking
ship, you know. You may say that I'm cynical,
my dear, but I think you'll find that I'm telling
you the facts as they are."

"It seems an awful insult to the woman to
send her a copy of your will," said Lady Johnstone.

"It's an awful insult to you when she tries
to get rid of her husband to marry your only
son, my dear."

"Oh — but he'd never marry her ! "

"I'm not sure. If he thought it would be
dishonourable not to marry her, he'd be quite

capable of doing it, and of blowing out his brains afterwards."

"That wouldn't improve her position," observed the practical Lady Johnstone.

"She'd be the widow of an honest man, instead of the wife of a blackguard," said Sir Adam. "However, I'm doing this on my own responsibility. What I want is that you should witness the will."

"And let Mrs. Crosby think I made you do this? No —"

"Nonsense. I sha'n't copy the signatures —"

"Then why do you need them at all?"

"I'm not going to write to her that I've made a will, if I haven't," answered Sir Adam. "A will isn't a will unless it's witnessed. I'm not going to lie about it, just to frighten her. So I want you and Mrs. Bowring to witness it."

"Mrs. Bowring?"

"Yes — there are no men here, and Brook can't be a witness, because he's interested. You and Mrs. Bowring will do very well. But there's another thing — rather an extraordinary thing — and I won't let you sign with her until you know it. It's not a very easy thing to tell you, my dear."

Lady Johnstone shifted her fat hands and folded them again, and her frank blue eyes gazed at her husband for a moment.

Lady Johnstone leaned back in her chair and slowly turned her head.
—*Page* 267.

"I can guess," she said, with a good-natured smile. "You told me you were old friends — I suppose you were in love with her somewhere!" She laughed and shook her head. "I don't mind," she added. "It's one more, that's all — one that I didn't know of. She's a very nice woman, and I've taken the greatest fancy to her!"

"I'm glad you have," said Sir Adam, gravely. "I say, my dear — don't be surprised, you know — I warned you. We knew each other very well — it's not what you think at all, and she was altogether in the right and I was quite in the wrong about it. I say, now — don't be startled — she's my divorced wife — that's all."

"She! Mrs. Bowring! Oh, Adam — how could you treat her so!"

Lady Johnstone leaned back in her chair and slowly turned her head till she could look out of the window. She was almost rosy with surprise — a change of colour in her sanguine complexion which was equivalent to extreme pallor in other persons. Sir Adam looked at her affectionately.

"What an awfully good woman you are!" he exclaimed, in genuine admiration.

"I! No, I'm not good at all. I was thinking that if you hadn't been such a brute to her I could never have married you. I don't sup-

pose that is good, is it? But you were a brute,
all the same, Adam, dear, to hurt such a woman
as that!"

"Of course I was! I told you so when I
told you the story. But I didn't expect that
you'd ever meet."

"No, it is an extraordinary thing. I suppose
that if I had any nerves I should faint. It
would be an awful thing if I did; you'd have to
get those porters to pick me up!" She smiled
meditatively. "But I haven't fainted, you see.
And, after all, I don't see why it should be so
very dreadful, do you? You see, you've rather
broken me in to the idea of lots of other people
in your life, and I've always pitied her sincerely.
I don't see why I should stop pitying her because
I've met her and taken such a fancy to her without knowing who she was. Do you?"

"Most women would," observed Sir Adam.
"It's lucky that you and she happen to be the
two best women in the world. I told Brook so
this morning."

"Brook? Have you told him?"

"I had to. He wants to marry her daughter."

"Brook! It's impossible!"

Lady Johnstone's tone betrayed so much more
surprise and displeasure than when her husband
had told her of Mrs. Bowring's identity that he
stared at her in surprise.

"I don't see why it's impossible," he said, "except that she has refused him once. That's nothing. The first time doesn't count."

"He sha'n't!" said the fat lady, whose vivid colour had come back. "He'll make her miserable — just as you — no, I won't say that! But they are not in the least suited to one another — he's far too young; there are fifty reasons."

"Brook won't act as I did, my dear," said Sir Adam. "He's like you in that. He'll make as good a husband as you have been a good wife —"

"Nonsense!" interrupted Lady Johnstone. "You're all alike, you Johnstones! I was talking to him this morning about her — I knew there was the beginning of something — and I told him what I thought. You're all bad, and I love you all; but if you think that Clare Bowring is as practical as I am, you're very much mistaken, Adam, dear! She'll break her heart —"

"If she does, I'll shoot him," answered the old man with a grim smile. "I told him so."

"Did you? Well, I am glad you take that view of it," said Lady Johnstone, thoughtfully, and not at all realising what she was saying. "I'm glad I'm not a nervous woman," she added, beginning to fan herself. "I should be in my grave, you know."

"No — you are not nervous, my dear, and

I'm very glad of it. I suppose it really is rather a trying situation. But if I didn't know you, I wouldn't have told you all this. You've spoiled me, you know — you really have been so tremendously good to me — always, dear."

There was a rough, half unwilling tenderness in his voice, and his big bony hand rested gently on the fat lady's shoulder, as he spoke. She bent her head to one side, till her large red cheek touched the brown knuckles. It was, in a way, almost grotesque. But there was that something in it which could make youth and beauty and passion ridiculous — the outspoken truthful old rake and the ever-forgiving wife. Who shall say wherein pathos lies? And yet it seems to be something more than a mere hack-writer's word, after all. The strangest acts of life sometimes go off in such an oddly quiet humdrum way, and then all at once there is the little quiver in the throat, when one least expects it — and the sad-eyed, faithful, loving angel has passed by quickly, low and soft, his gentle wings just brushing the still waters of our unwept tears.

Sir Adam left his wife to go in search of Mrs. Bowring. He sent a message to her, and she came out and met him in the corridor. They went into the reading-room together, and he shut the door. In a few words he told her all

In a few words he told her all he had told his wife about Mrs. Crosby.
— *Page* 270.

that he had told his wife about Mrs. Crosby, and asked her whether she had any objection to signing the document as a witness, merely in order that he might satisfy himself by actually executing it.

"It is high handed," said Mrs. Bowring. "It is like you—but I suppose you have a right to save your son from such trouble. But there is something else — do you know what has happened? He has been making love to Clare — he has asked her to marry him, and she has refused. She told me this morning — and I have told her the truth — that you and I were once married."

She paused, and watched Sir Adam's furrowed face.

"I'm glad of that," he said. "I'm glad that it has all come out on the same day. He knows everything, and he has told me everything. I don't know how it's all going to end, but I want you to believe one thing. If he had guessed the truth, he would never have said a word of love to her. He's not that kind of boy. You do believe me, don't you?"

"Yes, I believe you. But the worst of it is that she cares for him too — in a way I can't understand. She has some reason, or she thinks she has, for disliking him, as she calls it. She wouldn't tell me. But she cares for him all the

same. She has told him, though she won't tell
me. There is something horrible in the idea of
our children falling in love with each other."

Mrs. Bowring spoke quietly, but her pale face
and nervous mouth told more than her words.

Sir Adam explained to her shortly what had
happened on the first evening after Brook's
arrival, and how Clare had heard it all, sitting
in the shadow just above the platform. Mrs.
Bowring listened in silence, covering her eyes
with her hands. There was a long pause after
he had finished speaking, but still she said
nothing.

"I should like him to marry her," said Sir
Adam at last, in a low voice.

She started and looked at him uneasily, remembering how well she had once loved him,
and how he had broken her heart when she was
young. He met her eyes quietly.

"You don't know him," he said. "He loves
her, and he will be to her — what I wasn't to
you."

"How can you say that he loves her? Three
weeks ago he loved that Mrs. Crosby."

"He? He never cared for her — not even at
first."

"He was all the more heartless and bad to
make her think that he did."

"She never thought so, for a moment. She

wanted my money, and she thought that she could catch him."

"Perhaps — I saw her, and I did not like her face. She had the look of an adventuress about her. That doesn't change the main facts. Your son and she were — flirting, to say the least of it, three weeks ago. And now he thinks himself in love with my daughter. It would be madness to trust such a man — even if there were not the rest to hinder their marriage. Adam — I told you that I forgave you. I have forgiven you — God knows. But you broke my life at the beginning like a thread. You don't know all there has been to forgive — indeed, you don't. And you are asking me to risk Clare's life in your son's hands, as I risked mine in yours. It's too much to ask."

"But you say yourself that she loves him."

"She cares for him — that was what I said. I don't believe in love as I did. You can't expect me to."

She turned her face away from him, but he saw the bitterness in it, and it hurt him. He waited a moment before he answered her.

"Don't visit my sins on your daughter, Lucy," he said at last. "Don't forget that love was a fact before you and I were born, and will be a fact long after we are dead. If these two love each other, let them marry. I hope that Clare

T

is like you, but don't take it for granted that
Brook is like me. He's not. He's more like
his mother."

"And your wife?" said Mrs. Bowring suddenly. "What would she say to this?"

"My wife," said Sir Adam, "is a practical
woman."

"I never was. Still — if I knew that Clare
loved him — if I could believe that he could love
her faithfully — what could I do? I couldn't
forbid her to marry him. I could only pray
that she might be happy, or at least that she
might not break her heart."

"You would probably be heard, if anybody is.
And a man must believe in God to explain your
existence," added Sir Adam, in a gravely medi-
tative tone. "It's the best argument I know."

CHAPTER XIV

BROOK JOHNSTONE had gone to his room when he had left his father, and was hastily packing his belongings, for he had made up his mind to leave Amalfi at once without consulting anybody. It is a special advantage of places where there is no railway that one can go away at a moment's notice, without waiting tedious hours for a train. Brook did not hesitate, for it seemed to him the only right thing to do, after Clare's refusal, and after what his father had told him. If she had loved him, he would have stayed in spite of every opposition. If he had never been told her mother's history, he would have stayed and would have tried to make her love him. As it was, he set his teeth and said to himself that he would suffer a good deal rather than do anything more to win the heart of Mrs. Bowring's daughter. He would get over it somehow in the end. He fancied Clare's horror if she should ever know the truth, and his fear of hurting her was as strong as his love. He made no phrases to himself, and he thought of nothing theatrical which he should like to say. He just set his teeth and packed his clothes alone. Possibly he swore rather unmercifully at the coat which would not fit into the right place, and at the starched shirt-cuffs which would not lie flat until he smashed them out of shape with unsteady hands.

When he was ready, he wrote a few words to Clare. He said that he was going away immediately, and that it would be very kind of her to let him say good-bye. He sent the note by a servant, and waited in the corridor at a distance from her door.

A moment later she came out, very pale.

"You are not really going, are you?" she asked, with wide and startled eyes. "You can't be in earnest?"

"I'm all ready," he answered, nodding slowly. "It's much better. I only wanted to say good-bye, you know. It's awfully kind of you to come out."

"Oh — I wouldn't have — " but she checked herself, and glanced up and down the long corridor. "We can't talk here," she added.

"It's so hot outside," said Brook, remembering how she had complained of the heat an hour earlier.

"Oh no — I mean — it's no matter. I'd rather go out for a moment."

She began to walk towards the door while she was speaking. They reached it in silence, and went out into the blazing sun. Clare had Brook's note still in her hand, and held it up to shield the glare from the side of her face as they crossed the platform. Then she realised that she had brought him to the very spot whereon he had said good-bye to Lady Fan. She stopped, and he stood still beside her.

" Not here," she said.

" No — not here," he answered.

" There's too much sun — really," said she, as the colour rose faintly in her cheeks.

" It's only to say good-bye," Brook answered sadly. " I shall always remember you just as you are now — with the sun shining on your hair."

It was so bright that it dazzled him as he looked. In spite of the heat she did not move, and their eyes met.

" Mr. Johnstone," Clare began, " please stay. Please don't let me feel that I have sent you away." There was a shade of timidity in the tone, and the eyes seemed brave enough to say something more. Brook hesitated.

" Well — no — it isn't that exactly. I've heard something — my father has told me something since I saw you — "

He stopped short and looked down.

"What have you heard?" she asked. "Something dreadful about us?"

"About us all — about him, principally. I can't tell you. I really can't."

"About him — and my mother? That they were married and separated?"

The steady innocent eyes had waited for him to look up again. He started as he heard her words.

"You don't mean to say that you know it too?" he cried. "Who has dared to tell you?"

"My mother — she was quite right. It's wrong to hide such things — she ought to have told me at once. Why shouldn't I have known it?"

"Doesn't it seem horrible to you? Don't you dislike me more than ever?"

"No. Why should I? It wasn't your fault. What has it to do with you? Or with me? Is that the reason why you are going away so suddenly?"

Brook stared at her in surprise, and the dawn of returning gladness was in his face for a moment.

"We have a right to live, whatever they did in their day," said Clare. "There is no reason why you should go away like this, at a moment's notice."

With an older woman he would have under-

" Won't you say good-bye to me?" he asked unsteadily. — *Page* 279.

stood the first time, but he did not dare to understand Clare, nor to guess that there was anything to be understood.

"Of course we have a right to live," he answered, in a constrained tone. "But that does not mean that I may stay here and make your life a burden. So I'm going away. It was quite different before I knew all this. Please don't stay out here — you'll get a sunstroke. I only wanted to say good-bye."

Man-like, having his courage at the striking-point, he wished to get it all over quickly and be off. The colour sank from Clare's face again, and she stood quite still for a moment, looking at him. "Good-bye," he said, holding out his hand, and trying hard to smile a little.

Clare looked at him still, but her hand did not meet his, though he waited, holding it out to her. Her face hardened as though she were making an effort, then softened again, and still he waited.

"Won't you say good-bye to me?" he asked unsteadily.

She hesitated a moment longer.

"No!" she answered suddenly. "I—I can't!"

And here the story comes to its conclusion, as many stories out of the lives of men and women seem to end at what is only their turning-point. For real life has no conclusion but real death, and that is a sad ending to a tale, and one which may as well be left to the imagination when it is possible.

Stories of strange things, which really occur, very rarely have what used to be called a " moral " either. All sorts of things happen to people who afterwards go on living just the same, neither much better nor much worse than they were in the beginning. The story is a slice, as it were, cut from the most interesting part of a life, generally at the point where that life most closely touches another, so that the future of the two momentarily depends upon each separately, and upon both together. The happiness or unhappiness of both, for a long time to come, is founded upon the action of each just at those moments. And sometimes, as in the tale here told, the least promising of all the persons concerned is the one who helps matters out. The only logical thing about life is the certainty that it must end. If there were any logic at all about what goes between birth and death, men would have found it out long ago, and we should all know how to live as soon as we leave school; whereas we spend our lives under Fate's ruler, trying to understand, while she raps us over the knuckles every other minute because we cannot learn our lesson and sit up straight, and be good without being prigs, and do right without sticking it through other people's peace of mind as one sticks a pin through a butterfly.

CASA BRACCIO.

BY

F. MARION CRAWFORD.

WITH THIRTEEN FULL-PAGE ILLUSTRATIONS FROM DRAWINGS
BY CASTAIGNE.

Buckram. 2 vols., in box. $2.00.

PRESS COMMENTS.

" Mr. Crawford's latest novel, 'Casa Braccio,' may not improbably come
to be regarded as the supreme masterpiece in fiction — of the English tongue
at least — that has appeared since ' Daniel Deronda.' Its breadth of human
emotion, its vividness of individualities, its splendor of coloring, all entitle
this novel to a lasting place in the literature of fiction." — *Chicago Inter-
Ocean.*

" Mr. Crawford has won success in two different fields of fiction. In this,
his present work, he combines these fields, and wins a greater success than
ever. There is but little question that ' Casa Braccio ' will prove to be the
great novel of the year." — *Boston Daily Advertiser.*

" We are grateful when Mr. Crawford keeps to his Italy. The poetry
and enchantment of the land are all his own, and ' Casa Braccio ' gives
promise of being his masterpiece. . . . He has the life, the beauty, the
heart and the soul of Italy at the tips of his fingers." — *Los Angeles Express.*

" Admirably strong and impressive." — *Boston Beacon.*

" From all points of view ' Casa Braccio ' is the most artistically finished,
dramatic, and powerful work Mr. Crawford has produced." — *New York
World.*

" The people who are fond of prating about the thinness of American
novels should read ' Casa Braccio,' for it is rich in all the qualities that go to
make up a good story. . . . It is safe to say that any one who reads one or
two of Crawford's stories will extend his acquaintance with this singularly
versatile and charming writer." — *San Francisco Chronicle.*

MACMILLAN & CO.,

66 FIFTH AVENUE, NEW YORK.

THE RALSTONS.

A Sequel to "Katharine Lauderdale."

BY

F. MARION CRAWFORD.

2 vols. 16mo. Cloth. $2.00.

PRESS COMMENTS.

"The interest is unflagging throughout. Never has the author done more brilliant, artistic work than here." — *Ohio State Journal.*

"It is immensely entertaining; once in the full swing of the narrative, one is carried on quite irresistibly to the end. The style throughout is easy and graceful, and the text abounds in wise and witty reflections on the realities of existence." — *Boston Beacon.*

"The book is admirably written; it contains passages full of distinction; it is instinct with intensity of purpose; the characters are drawn with a living touch." — *London Daily News.*

"Mr. Crawford's new story, 'The Ralstons,' is as powerful a work as any that has come from his pen. . . . Harmonized by a strength and warmth of imagination uncommon in modern fiction, the story will be heartily enjoyed by every one who reads it." — *Edinburgh Scotsman.*

"As a picture of a certain kind of New York life, it is correct and literal; as a study of human nature, it is realistic enough to be modern, and romantic enough to be of the age of Trollope."—*Chicago Herald.*

"The whole group of character studies is strong and vivid." — *Literary World.*

"Mr. Crawford's pen portraits are wonderfully vivid. His analysis of motive is keen and subtle. His portrayal of passion, be it love or avarice, is most graphic." — *Boston Advertiser.*

MACMILLAN & CO.,

66 FIFTH AVENUE, NEW YORK.

SARACINESCA.

SANT' ILARIO.

A sequel to "Saracinesca."

DON ORSINO.

A continuation of "Saracinesca" and "Sant' Ilario."

MACMILLAN & CO.,

66 FIFTH AVENUE, NEW YORK.

WITH THE IMMORTALS.

MARZIO'S CRUCIFIX.

KHALED.

A Story of Arabia.

PAUL PATOFF.

MACMILLAN & CO.,

66 FIFTH AVENUE, NEW YORK.

A CIGARETTE-MAKER'S ROMANCE.

"It is a touching romance, filled with scenes of great dramatic power."
— *Boston Commercial Bulletin.*
"It is full of life and movement, and is one of the best of Mr. Crawford's books." — *Boston Saturday Evening Gazette.*
"The interest is unflagging throughout. Never has Mr. Crawford done more brilliant realistic work than here. But his realism is only the case and cover for those intense feelings which, placed under no matter what humble conditions, produce the most dramatic and the most tragic situations. . . . This is a secret of genius, to take the most coarse and common material, the meanest surroundings, the most sordid material prospects, and out of the vehement passions which sometimes dominate all human beings to build up with these poor elements scenes and passages, the dramatic and emotional power of which at once enforce attention and awaken the profoundest interest." — *New York Tribune.*

GREIFENSTEIN.

"'Greifenstein' is a remarkable novel, and while it illustrates once more the author's unusual versatility, it also shows that he has not been tempted into careless writing by the vogue of his earlier books. . . . There is nothing weak or small or frivolous in the story. The author deals with tremendous passions working at the height of their energy. His characters are stern, rugged, determined men and women, governed by powerful prejudices and iron conventions, types of a military people, in whom the sense of duty has been cultivated until it dominates all other motives, and in whom the principle of 'noblesse oblige' is, so far as the aristocratic class is concerned, the fundamental rule of conduct. What such people may be capable of is startlingly shown." — *New York Tribune.*

A ROMAN SINGER.

"One of Mr. Crawford's most charming stories — a love romance pure and simple." — *Boston Home Journal.*
"'A Roman Singer' is one of his most finished, compact, and successful stories, and contains a splendid picture of Italian life." — *Toronto Mail.*

MACMILLAN & CO.,
66 FIFTH AVENUE, NEW YORK.

THE THREE FATES.

"The strength of the story lies in its portrayal of the aspirations, disciplinary efforts, trials, and triumphs of the man who is a born writer, and who, by long and painful experiences, learns the good that is in him and the way in which to give it effectual expression. The analytical quality of the book is excellent, and the individuality of each one of the very dissimilar three fates is set forth in an entirely satisfactory manner. . . . Mr. Crawford has manifestly brought his best qualities as a student of human nature and his finest resources as a master of an original and picturesque style to bear upon this story. Taken for all in all it is one of the most pleasing of all his productions in fiction, and it affords a view of certain phases of American, or perhaps we should say of New York, life that have not hitherto been treated with anything like the same adequacy and felicity." — *Boston Beacon.*

CHILDREN OF THE KING.

A Tale of Southern Italy.

"A sympathetic reader cannot fail to be impressed with the dramatic power of this story. The simplicity of nature, the uncorrupted truth of a soul, have been portrayed by a master-hand. The suddenness of the unforeseen tragedy at the last renders the incident of the story powerful beyond description. One can only feel such sensations as the last scene of the story incites. It may be added that if Mr. Crawford has written some stories unevenly, he has made no mistakes in the stories of Italian life. A reader of them cannot fail to gain a clearer, fuller acquaintance with the Italians and the artistic spirit that pervades the country." — M. L. B. in *Syracuse Journal.*

THE WITCH OF PRAGUE.

A Fantastic Tale.

ILLUSTRATED BY W. J. HENNESSY.

"'The Witch of Prague' is so remarkable a book as to be certain of as wide a popularity as any of its predecessors. The keenest interest for most readers will lie in its demonstration of the latest revelations of hypnotic science. . . . It is a romance of singular daring and power." — *London Academy.*

"Mr. Crawford has written in many keys, but never in so strange a one as that which dominates 'The Witch of Prague.' . . . The artistic skill with which this extraordinary story is constructed and carried out is admirable and delightful. . . . Mr. Crawford has scored a decided triumph, for the interest of the tale is sustained throughout. . . . A very remarkable, powerful, and interesting story." — *New York Tribune.*

MACMILLAN & CO.,

66 FIFTH AVENUE, NEW YORK.

ZOROASTER.

"The field of Mr. Crawford's imagination appears to be unbounded. . . . In 'Zoroaster' Mr. Crawford's winged fancy ventures a daring flight. . . . Yet 'Zoroaster' is a novel rather than a drama. It is a drama in the force of its situations and in the poetry and dignity of its language; but its men and women are not men and women of a play. By the naturalness of their conversation and behavior they seem to live and lay hold of our human sympathy more than the same characters on a stage could possibly do." — *The Times.*

A TALE OF A LONELY PARISH.

"It is a pleasure to have anything so perfect of its kind as this brief and vivid story. . . . It is doubly a success, being full of human sympathy, as well as thoroughly artistic in its nice balancing of the unusual with the commonplace, the clever juxtaposition of innocence and guilt, comedy and tragedy, simplicity and intrigue." — *Critic.*
"Of all the stories Mr. Crawford has written, it is the most dramatic, the most finished, the most compact. . . . The taste which is left in one's mind after the story is finished is exactly what the fine reader desires and the novelist intends. . . . It has no defects. It is neither trifling nor trivial. It is a work of art. It is perfect." — *Boston Beacon.*

MARION DARCHE.

"Full enough of incident to have furnished material for three or four stories. . . . A most interesting and engrossing book. Every page unfolds new possibilities, and the incidents multiply rapidly." — *Detroit Free Press.*
"We are disposed to rank 'Marion Darche' as the best of Mr. Crawford's American stories." — *The Literary World.*

AN AMERICAN POLITICIAN.

THE NOVEL: What It Is.

18mo. Cloth. 75 Cents.

"When a master of his craft speaks, the public may well listen with careful attention, and since no fiction-writer of the day enjoys in this country a broader or more enlightened popularity than Marion Crawford, his explanation of 'The Novel: What It Is,' will be received with flattering interest." — *The Boston Beacon.*

MACMILLAN & CO.,
66 FIFTH AVENUE, NEW YORK.